THE SAVIOUR
NEVER LETS HER GO

AVINASH AGARWAL

www.novelavinash.com

www.facebook.com/thesaviourneverletshergo

First published in Great Britain in 2015 by

Createspace publishing, an Amazon company

Cover design by Diana Buidoso/Dienel96

ISBN-10:1518882536
ISBN-13:978-1518882531

DEDICATION

I would like to dedicate this book to my father, Mr. Madhukar Agarwal, as my destiny would have been different without his influence in my life.

ACKNOWLEDGMENTS

I am indebted to many individuals who have helped me throughout this wonderful journey of writing. Nothing to do with tradition, but first let me thank my loving wife Prachi who has supported me in many ways, and my adorable sons, Aryan and Aman, who have been so patient while I spent countless evenings and weekends to fulfil my dream of writing this book. Thanks a ton to Pragya who provided brilliant suggestions and stood her grounds while arguing on various iterations. Much appreciate the information my dear friend Rajan provided me in the early days of writing this fiction. Thanks a bunch to Steve and everyone who read my book and provided valuable feedback.

EPIGRAPH

He insulted me, he cheated me, he robbed me' – those who are free of resentful thoughts surely find peace.

Buddha; 568-488 BC, Founder of Buddhism

Contents

1. Ceremony

"Tomorrow will be the beginning of our medical career", Joe sighed with relief and a sense of exaltation. He relaxed on a large couch keeping his legs stretched outright.

The living room was good size. The painting on the left wall was showing light colours, mostly sky blue and grey, signifying the winter. The centre piece was a giant tree with a thick trunk but without a leaf. Its thousands of branches spread out like arms gathering the sky, and its giant roots like ready to swallow the earth. The painting on the right wall was showing bright colours, mostly red and yellow, representing a sunny day. The centre piece being the similar giant tree but with dark green leaves, celebrating the summer and vitality. The trees in both the paintings were as if symbolising the ups and downs of life. The contrast of the paintings was created by none other than the owner of the house, Reeve Harvey – precisely, Dr. Reeve Harvey.

"Yes, in a way - life is all about beginnings", Reeve muttered.

He seemed worn out after a long swimming session. Sitting on a couch opposite to Joe, his cold hazel eyes looked away. His classic square shaped face, with a strong jaw line, was a matrix of contrast features – contemptuous yet considerate; confident yet naive; simple yet firm. He looked like a slayer or a bodyguard.

"It's NOT going to be a piece of cake, I guess! I mean, you know, these days a doctor has to be much more careful about everything." Joe chatted away.

"Hmm, you think so?!" Reeve said softly.

"Did you not see the news yesterday on tele about a patient who has sued his doctor for not warning him for his obesity? And, as if it was not way over the top, the doctor has been charged for the misconduct! Personally, I think it's ludicrous. Though, it would have been nice to give advice but how can you make someone change their way of lives or be responsible for what they are?!" Joe was excited.

"That's the way it is - we have to learn to be more responsible, I suppose", Reeve replied.

"And there is no end to it until people learn to be responsible for themselves", Joe shrugged.

"Quite right."

"Tell me one thing - would you trust me, if, I found myself in a situation where I can't prove myself? Joe asked his best friend.

"I would think so. In a life there are always ups and downs but our downfall should always give us the force to go even higher like a tennis ball which goes as high as hard you throws on the ground".

"Right, but some doctors really do give shame to their profession, don't they? I mean, look at Dr. Sharman's case who abused his young patients?" Ever-enquiring Joe said.

"I don't think about it."

"What do you mean? Don't you condemn him? Joe was mystified.

Reeve had nothing to say and looked away. *There are things one must not observe; even the thoughts of it can erode the purity, the sacredness, of one's own actions; one's own thoughts. Moral has a limit to its demise and beyond that, neither it can be remorse nor can be punished enough. And, mere the knowledge of its ugliness makes you feel ashamed, guilty and conscious of being a human - a human with highest power of judgment of morality; a human with longest history of civilization; the greatest creator on the earth.* He thought.

That day, they were to be awarded the 'Bachelor of Medicine and Bachelor of Surgery' degree. The graduation ceremony of New London Medical College was a grand, colourful and cultural event. Juniors had organized an evening with a well-known pop singer, besides other entertaining programs throughout the day for everyone's entertainment.

Reeve was wearing a black hood and a navy blue gown – blue, the colour of heaven; the most 'pure' of the primary colours. Perhaps a symbol of purity of the task ahead of him.

Mr. William Harvey sat in his wheelchair near his daughter in a big ceremony hall.

The first speech was given by the Chancellor of the College, Mr. Rudd Sharman. After the speeches, certificates were to be handed over followed by the entertaining events.

The names were being announced individually. "Mr. Joe Ferguson", the name was announced. Joe ascended the stairs and met the Chancellor to receive his certificate. Shortly after that, Reeve's name was announced.

Reeve's dad, William Harvey, applauded with the audience. He was not a very old man but appeared to have seen a great deal of life.

Reeve glanced at his father and sister who were looking at him.

Tears dropped down William's face. They were tears of happiness and pride; of guilt and lost moments. *Somebody has rightly said, everybody is a sinner in one way or another,* William Harvey thought.

2. Tsunami

Joe reached for his certificate a fourth times since he received it gracefully two days back, and every time he held it, he felt a sense of thrill and achievement. He had fulfilled his childhood dream. He felt as if he was dreaming about something the whole night and when he woke up in the morning, he saw that a night angel has fulfilled his wish. His enthusiasm was fuelled by the speech given by the dean of NLMC on the first day of his joining. The words of Mr. Howard Kent have had echoed in his mind, time and again; "I am delighted to welcome you to New London Medical College as you embark on your career in medicine. NLMC has the faculty, curriculum, facilities and clinical affiliates to provide you with the first class 21st century medical education to produce the best physicians and scientists. We can expect extraordinary advances in understanding of medical sciences and the new approaches to treatment and diagnosis. Nevertheless, the focus of your career will always be on being a good doctor whom a patient can talk to and trust and who will practice medicine with the highest ethical standards. I hope that you will continue to deepen your sense of compassion for people and honesty for others – not only in medical practice but in all your endeavours. My best wishes…"

A journey, he had started five years ago in New London Medical College, had been full of challenges - overwhelming and sometimes even terrifying - and now it had taken a new turn as he prepared to start on his training as pre-registration house officers (PRHOs). Though, his parents were delighted to see him as a doctor, it was his own resolution to become a doctor and Fergusons had always encouraged him to choose what he truly and truthfully wanted to do in his life. Perhaps it was his upbringing and the experiences he has had that led him choose his career.

Almost thirty years back, when his father, Dr. Derek Ferguson, had planned his holidays in Kenya at the age of 32, with his fiancée Liz, little did they know that it was going to be their home for the next twelve years. That was an unprecedentedly long and life changing holiday for them.

When they arrived at Moi International Airport of Mombasa, it was almost 33 hours since they left their home in South London. They needed some rest before they could start exploring the city. For the next three days, they had planned to see Mombasa; an ancient city built on an Island and connected to mainland by a land bridge. Around 2000 years back Mombasa used to be the centre of trade and communication between East Africa, Middle East and Far East countries.

The next day, they hired a cab to see the city and the first destination they arrived at was Fort Jesus; a dominating figure located on the edge of a coral ridge overlooking the entrance to the Old Port of Mumbasa built by the Portuguese to signify their reign on the East African Coast. It was also used as a prison when Kenya was made a British Colony.

On the third day, when their cab didn't turn up even after an hour long wait, they dared to take a ride on a "Matatu" - a brightly painted, popular mode of transport, used by locals. They arrived at a "Matatu" stop for downtown trip to Mombasa.

"Mzungu, come here – come here", a young "Matatu" conductor, wearing a bucket hat and the required uniform, colours albeit in trendy style, shouted. Two other Matatus approached at the same time to get to the paying customers first, side by side, hogging the road…a scene one can mistake for a stampede. Derek and Liz were dragged in by the flow of waiting passengers and squeezed up into the belly of a 24-seater minibus. There was barely standing room inside, Derek and Liz stood facing each other with nothing to hold on but the bodies of people standing around them simply pressed against them. It was like a tight bottle of soft beetroot rings pressed against each other. "Are you OK", Derek asked Liz knowing well that she wasn't - not then. But all she could hear was the deafening sound of the African reggae music, being played by a powerful hi-fi system. She could feel the decibels vibrating into her eardrums helping to numb her senses. The smells and sounds of the people around them was a new experience to their senses. It was an experience of a world they never knew existed. The ride came to a screeching halt after a breath-taking experience and they stepped down slowly. The conductor smiled at Derek and said "Baadaye (see you later)."

"Asante (thank you)", Derek managed to say.

"That was quite an adventure", Liz said with a sigh of relief.

"Yes, an adventure you can't experience on any ride in Blackpool or Disneyland!"

The day was long and busy and by the time, they got back in their hotel, they both were exhausted. By then, they had seen almost all the attractions in the town and they decided to spend the rest of their holiday, soaking up the sun on white sandy beaches.

It was 9 O'clock in the morning when Derek looked down from the balcony of his exclusive suite on the first floor of his hotel which was situated on the north coast of Mombasa. The white sandy beach, fringed by coconut trees and coral reefs, was shining in the sun, as if, the large sea front was wearing a golden necklace, embellished with coloured gemstones. The heat from the sun was being cooled down by gentle sea-breezes. It was a paradise which would have calmed the senses of the most nervous person. He felt a sense of joy and blessed – blessed, that he could come here.

"Let's have breakfast and then go to the beach to make most of this sunshine" Derek said.

"Sure! But don't forget to use sunblock and your shades, before you go out." Liz instructed.

It was a breathlessly hot morning and the sea was calm and benevolent. They spent the next three hours relaxing on the beach before returning to their room to have a meal. Derek wanted to go back to the beach after the meal but Liz had a sudden urge to stay in the hotel and instead view the beautiful beach from the balcony. On the coast line, there were several small hotels, restaurant & cafes, where people were enjoying food with their families. Street vendors were selling ice cream, drinks, fish and a variety of snacks including a deep fried pastry triangle stuffed with spicy minced meat called Sambusas and Mkate Mayai, a folded thin pancake made of wheat dough and filled with raw egg and minced meat. By that time, strong winds were bringing the kind of crashing waves that were delighting the wind-surfers. There were few small and long boats in the water carrying fishermen. The beach was full of men, women and children who were enjoying the sun, sand and sea. The kids were playing on the shore, wearing water jackets. Some kids were making sand sculptures or flying giant kites. There were teens playing football and volleyball. A few people were busy capturing moments of their happy times and every inch of such a beautiful place in their little memory boxes called cameras.

"It's great to see how much people are enjoying there", Liz said brightly.

"Yes, but can you see what I am seeing?" Derek asked with his eyes wide open.

"What are you talk-." Derek interrupted her before she could finish.

"Can you see far down the sea - that white wall coming towards the shore?"

"Oh! Jesus! Its looks like a tsunami?" she almost shouted with a shocking realization.

"I must go downstairs and start warning people"

"Wait! There is no time for that. See - people have already started realizing it."

"Yes. Oh! Look at that small boat – its flying up in the air!"

"Oh lord! Now its two walls of water moving up the bay. Can you see that?"

"It must be around fifteen to twenty feet high each."

It was a sudden panic which spread through the crowd on the beach, like a wild fire. Parents were pulling their children up, and running, leaving behind all their stuff - sensing the scarcity of the time. People were screaming for their kids and tourists, to get out and run away. The waves were now barely seconds away from the shore. A cruiser around fifty feet in the length went straight up in the air on the waves and landed upright. A few motorboats and long-tail boats were flipped over by the strong flow of water. The sea rose up like a giant dragon to swallow everything in its path. The dark brown water was spanning the horizon with no sign of remorse for anyone or anything. The water then rushed into the beachfront cafés, restaurants and buildings, wiping out the ground floor completely. The crashing sounds of the water, smashing the glasses, windows and furniture, were making the deafening noises. People floating in the water, like vegetables, were creating a scene of havoc. It was an utter devastation.

A journey from heaven to hell had been spanned only in a few seconds – a scene of people laughing, enjoying, playing and eating had been changed to a scene of people crying, dying and running for their lives. A few seconds later, a second wave came, larger than the first one and it caused even more devastation. A few people managed to get to the first floor in time but others had only time to cling to trees to survive. After the first wave, a father was still holding his four year old son from one hand and the tree from the other hand, but the second wave pulled them apart and drowned the son in a hotel swimming pool which was invisible as water surrounded the pool. Water continued splashing all over onto Derek and Liz, after crashing to the ground floor. They stood still, unable to move, to respond or to save anyone or anything.

Suddenly Derek realized about Liz and asked, "Are you alright?"

"Yes, I think so – I don't think any other big wave will come now so we should go downstairs and help."

"Are you sure you are OK, and don't want to rest?" Derek knew that it might not be easy for Liz to see this unprecedented catastrophe, especially when she was 16 weeks pregnant.

"Yes, I am."

"OK, I will get my bag - I should start helping them." Being a doctor, he always kept a first-aid kit with him.

After the second big wave, several smaller waves hit over the next few hours and each wave was gentler than the last one. The bay repeatedly drained and then refilled.

Derek and Liz came downstairs and began to look for people who were severely injured. Most of the people who were on the beach or ground floor were either dead or had injuries, cuts, bruises and knocks. Derek ran to a man, with his first-aid kit, who was in his forties and had his head injured with a lamp post while floated on the water.

A week after the tsunami, the death toll in Kenya rose to eight thousand, with several of people still missing or presumed dead.

Several temporary hospital camps were arranged to serve the injured people as hospitals were full of their capacity. Derek and Liz were actively participating in the relief program. There was an acute shortage of medical staff for the people affected by the tsunami. They felt a duty to serve them and somehow, they felt a sense of guilt about leaving Kenya as they were lucky to have survived, after seeing hundreds of people dying in front of their eyes. And then days became weeks and weeks became months before they realized that months have passed serving the affected people and participating in international relief programme.

"Do you like to stay here and want to continue or rather you would like to go back to England?" Derek asked Liz when she was almost 28 weeks pregnant.

"I think so - the weather is fine, the people are fantastic here and I love what I am doing, so we can continue, if you wish the same."

"Great! Same here. I will fax my resignation tomorrow and will apply for a job in some hospital here."

After a few weeks Liz gave birth to Joe, and Derek joined the Mombasa hospital on a mere eight thousand Kenyan Shillings a month. They stayed there for the next twelve years and then decided to move back to England to provide Joe a better education. It was as if Joe inherited his parents' virtue of serving mankind, thus wanted to become a doctor since his childhood.

3. Emotions

It was a quiet and beautiful river bank. Lying on his back, gazing towards the blue sky, he felt relaxed and pious, as if, all his senses were in the highest state of tranquillity.

And then moments later, hundreds of small massagers were massaging his body in a harmonized rhythm, and with the delicacy of a perfectionist. The contentment was beyond his imagination.

He was thrilled, astonished and then frightened. This place doesn't belong to my world. I must have lost my way, he thought. I was naked and tied with strong iron chains; my naked body was lying on the floor wrapped with fear and cold. The guard was lashing the leather whip mercilessly, without a count but with a sense of duty and panic. I was a slave – a slave of the people who enjoyed crushing the morale of the crusaders; the dignity of a human; the senses of the sensible and honesty of a true love.

Suddenly hundreds of those small massagers turned into monsters and rammed their tiny vicious weapons into his body. "Kill me or join me – I give you only two choices", he shouted with sheer pain and disgust. Then he woke up and threw his head high in the air above his knees and folded legs. He got up, walked and sat on a nearby rock. First, it was drizzling softly and then water droplets had started hammering hard on his naked body. The sky was suddenly covered with dark clouds. After a while, Reeve went home.

"Ding-Dong, Ding-Dong", the doorbell brought Joe back from his memories and he realized that he had fallen asleep with his memories of what her mother had told him. He reached to the door, moved the key into the slot and opened the door. Reeve entered with his usual faint smile which Joe termed a typical 'Mona Lisa' smile.

"Where have you been?" Joe enquired.

"I went for a swim."

"You have been quite secretive these days - are you dating somebody?" Joe chuckled.

"I don't want to date."

"You mean you don't like girls?"

"I didn't say that."

"So when do you think you would want to date?"

"I don't know, I never thought of it."

"Well I am just worried since I won't be staying here forever to advise you." Joe chuckled again.

"I don't need anybody. I don't seek love and it saves me suffering."

"Well Mr. Right! May be you can say that because you don't feel anything. Others are human, sensitive, and they feel; and they want to be loved. In a way, I think you are lucky, not to have any feelings. Others can't be like this."

He stood motionless, looking away and whispered, "Yes, I suppose I never felt anything."

After a while, he left the house; he didn't feel pain but sympathy for Joe – a sympathy for the suffering Joe was ready to take for this world. The flawed world.

Joe never understood Reeve. Whenever he had thought about him; he was left confused with a sense of serenity in his own way. How a person can be so understanding, modest and noble, yet so emotionless about the people who might be referred as his friends, colleagues, family, and acquaintances, he thought. His indifference for the people was almost shocking and inhumane. So, is he really so cold about everyone? No, I can't say that either. But how damn he could be in control of all the nerve cells of his mind and body – as if, he is incapable to love them; hate them or expect anything from them. Only thing he seems capable to resent is the incompetence of people and even that was so impersonal that made the subject forgetful and there was only an objective – The perfection. He contemplated.

Once in the middle of a casual conversation Joe had said, "I feel, I expect a lot from the people because I know I can give them more than they can."

"If you can give them what you can, then you should. It shouldn't matter what you get in return. What you give them is your virtue and what they'll give you is their virtue. One doesn't need to depend on others for their own acts and beliefs. When your own actions will be freed from any prejudice than only you can find true happiness. And your free will is nothing but the sensible image of infinite. Its purity and impartiality is the companion of the soul", Reeve had argued.

"You mean we should act like a robot" Joe chuckled.

"Sort of', if you can! The greatness of mankind lies in the ability to recognize the right and wrong programme. And his actions should be driven only by his own true consciousness and beliefs, like a robot, which is programmed to do the right things and who perform its duties, regardless of its owner, his behavior, color, character or clothing. When one's actions are outcome of other's actions then they behave like corrupted software or a virus infected computer, defying their own virtues and beliefs and working on impulse of others. Unfortunately, there is no Anti-virus software for humans which can be run to undo their misdeeds. Once dragged in the abyss of hate, jealousy, shame or anger beyond a point, there is no point of return. One only needs to act for oneself, what one think is right, and pleases his innermost like eternity. Only, if one can listen to oneself without caring for others, without being dependent on the actions of others."

Emotions are mankind's biggest hurdle and the evil in the way of happiness, he thought. They love some people but couldn't resist hating others. They feel proud for some, only to be jealous for others. They worry for some but do not care for others. Their emotions bring more sadness than happiness; more hatred than love; more prejudice than tolerance; and more destruction than creativity to mankind. The greatness of mankind is held slave of emotions. His idea of the freedom was the freedom of his own actions and his own emotions. The freedom to act upon the things that give satisfaction to nobody but to your inner self; to act to please your inner self only. That was the only way to happiness in life.

Emotions make people frail and senseless. Emotions have become a disease we must eradicate from this world and create new standards for human being where his actions will be based on his values; his beliefs; his virtues - not his emotions; his impulse. Emotions are damned in this world.

4. Love - A Fairy Tale

It was only in the third year of his medical degree when Joe had met Shirley during a medical congress on 'Respirology & the Infective Exacerbations' in London, while she was also in the third year her medical degree. Though, it was not the most pleasant meeting by any standard. Joe was walking between the rows of seats, to sit in middle of a row, to have a better view of the seminar. Then, a woman coming from the opposite direction had bumped into him, with her cup of tea. The tea was spilled all over his coat. "I am sorry, I am so sorry", she had pleaded with a real sense of guilt while taking out her handkerchief and trying to wipe his sapphire coat.

"It's OK, it's OK", Joe had replied, barely able to hide his frustration.

He looked at the woman who was in her thirties and was wearing round glasses. She had a sleek face and sharp features. She wore a raspberry print wrap dress with long sleeve and mock-wrap V-neckline with georgette drapes, tied at the side for a flattering fit. The woman was average looking, but the aura she has created around herself, by her confidence and elegance, made her glamorous.

They sat together and introduced each other. "I am Shirley Watson; doing my MBBS from Penchester University."

"I am Joe Ferguson; doing MBBS from New London Medical College."

"I think it's a wonderful opportunity to interact with so many distinguished clinicians and scientists present here, from all around the world," Shirley said, as she tried to break the ice. She felt bad about the incident and wanted to lighten up the atmosphere.

"Yes, that's right. Some of my colleagues will be showing posters of their clinical research here as well." Joe replied, feeling a bit better then. The seminar was about to start now and the first guest; Dr. John Lehman from New York Medical College arrived on the stage to share his expertise in respiratory medicine. Some two thousands international and local delegates were participating in this event held at London's Imperial Hotel convention centre. Later in the day, Shirley was surprised to find out that Joe himself had won the Best Poster Award in the 'Chronic obstructive Pulmonary Disease' category.

"You have done a great job on this," Shirley complimented him later, when she met him again during luncheon.

"I think, the real credit goes to our Professor, Dr. Thomas Mann – we did this study under his supervision," Joe replied.

Shirley bombarded him with quite a few questions about his poster and as if that wasn't enough, she said, "Probably, I would like to know more about your study some time,"

"Yes sure. Would you like to take my number?" Joe asked, taking out his mobile.

"Oh yes, please."

"Please tell me your number and I will give you a miss call so you can save my number."

"Sure, thanks!"

They exchanged their numbers and after a while they were talking as if they were childhood friends who have met each other after a long time. They were really seemed to be enjoying each other's company. Though, their colleagues, seniors and others kept coming to them during the event but they were like the South and North Pole of a magnet which can only be kept apart with a physical force and as soon as the force was gone, they would be pulled in towards each other.

Later, when Joe told her that he lived in Hounslow in London, somehow he looked pleased to know that Shirley visited the area frequently as her parent's lived there. The seminar ended with a useful sharing of the latest findings about the diseases and the advancement in medical technologies among the delegates from all over the world. They walked down to the car park together while Joe held his coat in his arm. It wasn't a very cold day so he could manage without the coat, besides it was dirty.

"I would like to invite you on a tea or a meal next week, if you can, when you visit your family in Hounslow," Joe asked.

"Oh! Thanks very much. I think I can make it. but on one condition!"

"Well, and what is that?"

"If you don't mind I can have your coat for dry cleaning and I'll return it when I'll see you next week."

"Oh no, no, you don't have to bother about that!"

"I know, but I insist – I will be happy if I can make up for something I have done."

He resisted but she was persistent.

"What can I say? If you are insisting – here it is," he handed over the coat to Shirley with a hint of smile.

"OK, then I will see you next Saturday then and I'll let you know the timing."

"Yes sure. And by the way, can I say - you are very considerate!"

"Oh! Thank you. See you later, bye."

"See you, bye."

He started the engine of his Peugeot 405 while watching Shirley who was slowly walking down to her car. Joe was surprised on how much ease he felt in her company despite all her confidence and elegance. When he first met her in the morning, he almost found her unattractive but now he actually liked her company, despite all the irritation he had towards her initially because of his new coat was spoiled which he bought last week from M&S. He was amused on the thought of Shirley as her next girlfriend and realized that she was different from all the girls he had met before. The only difference was that he didn't believe in love-in-first-sight any more. It never worked for him. Most of the time, it was only infatuation or mere physical attraction between opposite sex. He met and fell in love with some of the most beautiful girls, but when the fizz was out of the bottle he realized how shallow their characters were. In the past, he had a series of brief and not-so- brief relationships but it never really quite worked out for him for one reason or another. He had decided to take a break. But then he had met Tanya, his last ex-girlfriend, who always seemed interested in talking about the fancy gadgets, clothing and shopping. She was a happy big spender – with anybody who had deep pockets and was ready to shell out as much as she wanted. He was happy to get rid of her as she dumped him for a millionaire property developer, whom she met when they had gone together to view a property to buy for themselves. After the break-up, he couldn't believe himself that he actually thought of buying a property with her and living together. Many times, he thought of breaking up with Tanya as he knew it was a relationship of convenience but could not do so. May be it was his loneliness, and her convenience to spend his money, that kept them together. But he always felt that life is more beautiful with a person with whom he can truly love and relate to himself. For him, love was the essence of life and centre of it. Now, he didn't want to embark on a casual relationship. He wondered if today was his lucky day. In just a short duration he had seen a glimpse of everything he wanted in Shirley. She seemed more interested in talking about small things in life which most people seemed to ignore.

"Pom-Pom," a car horn sounded and Joe suddenly realized that he was still in the car park and was blocking the way of a car coming from his right side. He was too busy watching Shirley and thinking about her.

It had been two days since he met her but they hadn't called each other. Joe was feeling restless and found his fingers dialling her number but she was on voicemail – he left a message, "Um! Hi! This is Joy; hope you remember me– the Coat guy! I was just calling to see if you are alright; I hope you will be coming over here on this weekend as we talked. Alright then, see you later." He hung up with a sense of disappointment and hoped that she would call him back soon. After an hour the phone rang and he took a deep breathe out, before picking the receiver. It was indeed Shirley. "Hey Joy, how are you doing? You are not worrying about your coat, are you? – Just kidding," she said with a laugh.

"Hahaha! I am fine and what about you?"

They talked freely about their lives, family, studies, college and lot of other things which they hadn't talked to anybody for years.

When Shirley hung up and looked over to the wall clock. It was twenty past seven. She gasped in horror. She was twenty minutes late for her evening biology class which she used to give to her next street neighbour's kids for the last few months. She was amazed how time has just flown away on phone. She felt guilty on the thought of kids waiting for her to come and take the class. She picked the phone and dialled Walker's number to inform that she would be there within minutes.

Joe put the receiver down and relaxed on the couch. He suddenly felt full of energy; of happiness; of desire; of purpose in life, as if a fire on the brink of extinguishing had been given a life by a stream of fresh air. After that, he called her every night but made sure that he called her only after 9pm in the night, so that she doesn't have to hurry up for her tuitions.

Joe had invited her on a meal as he self-praised on his cooking skills. Joe was thinking about the Friday evening and suddenly he realized that Reeve didn't know that Shirley was coming over for a meal. Till then, he had avoided telling Reeve about Shirley. One reason was that he wasn't sure about their relationship yet, and the other was that Reeve didn't believe in relationships, as if, he never needed anyone in his life. He doesn't belong to this earth, he thought. But then he had to tell him that she would come the next day on dinner as he was sharing the house with him and wanted the odd man out!

"Um, sorry, I forgot to tell you that I met a girl in the last week's congress and she is coming over tomorrow evening for a dinner."

"Well, that was a quick arrangement," Reeve chuckled.

"Oh no, no, she is visiting her parents in Hounslow this weekend and I just invited her and got lucky – she accepted."

"Oh, yes of course."

"So do you have any plan for the evening – are you gonna be here?" Joe enquired.

"Oh yes, sure, if you don't mind."

"Oh no, no, I would be pleased if you join us". Joe said in a sarcastic way.

"I am only joking. I won't spoil your evening, would I? So what time she is coming?"

"Ah! Seven O'clock." Joe replied with a hint of smile.

"OK, I've some work, so I'll come late anyway but if I'll come; I would rather not disturb you."

"No, you won't disturb me!"

He started to cook chicken curry and rice. During their conversation, Shirley had told him that she likes chicken curry. He had planned about dinner days ahead and done lots of shopping the previous day. He opened a pack of frozen chicken breasts and put it onto the wooden board to slice into small pieces, covered them in a foil and left in the oven to cook. He then chopped the onions finely and fried it in a large frying pan until they got light brown and then he added tomatoes, coriander, black pepper and curry powder, and fried again for couple of minutes before pouring over chicken curry sauce and let it simmer on low heat for five minutes. Then he washed the rice in a big bowl. Being a smart cook, he knew how to manage the time in kitchen and within an hour he's prepared quite a few things but then most of the food was frozen or 'ready to cook', so he just had to make good use of all the kitchen appliances available at his disposal.

After finishing the cooking, he set the table in dining room with dishes, napkins and all the cutlery requirements. He put a crystal vase with fresh mixed of yellow, pink and red Freesia corms on the window sill which he bought specially for the evening. He checked the time - it was only quarter to seven and he still had time to see, if anything was not up to the mark. He had cleaned the carpets and house again that day even though Reeve had done it just a couple of days ago as he didn't want to appear messy on his first date with Shirley, besides he wanted to make her feel good. For him, it was a courtesy to have the place tidy for his guests so they feel welcome.

Shirley had not mentioned about her date to her parents. There is nothing serious, it's just that I am going to return his coat, she convinced herself. Besides, she knew that Anna would be far too interested to know everything about Joe, had she told her about him. I am not ready to divulge anything yet, she decided. She looked over to the wall clock which told her that still two hours were left for 7 PM. She picked the towel from the wet cloth stand and walked to the bathroom to take the shower and came out from the bathroom wrapped in the towel. She gave a glance to the clock on the wall and was shocked to realise that it was quarter to six. *It would take one hour to drive so I better hurry,* she thought. She picked the packet of dry cleaned coat which she had picked a day before while returning from college and ran to the front door. She unlocked the car and started the car engine but her back mind suggested that she had forgotten something. She had learned from experience that whenever she had a feeling that she had forgotten something she would have surely forgotten something. She turned off the engine and returned to the front room and took out a bottle of red wine from the cupboard which she had bought for Joe.

Joe was changing the CD when he heard the doorbell. He rushed to the door and found Shirley standing there and smiling at him. She was looking even more elegant than she looked when he first met her. She wore a black dress with stylish kabuki sleeves and a flattering empire waist tied at back. It had a surplice wrap front with floral lace inset. "Sorry I am a bit late; here is your coat," she kissed him on the cheek and handed over the packet.

He wore a short sleeve, navy blue cotton t-shirt with two button placket which complimented his stone coloured Levis jeans.

"Not a problem, at least you've come."

"So, you weren't sure that I was going to make it?" she smiled and followed him in the living room.

"No, I just thought you might change your mind or something". Joe said smilingly.

"Perceptions are always different from realities, I guess," she laughed and added, "Here, it's for you," she handed over the bottle of wine.

"Right! Dinner is ready – shall we proceed in the kitchen or you want to wait?

"Shall we go for dinner a bit later?"

"It's alright, I am not hungry yet." "I'll get you some wine though," Joe suggested.

"OK, I'll come with you." They walked down to the kitchen and Joe uncorked the wine bottle and poured it in the goblets and handed one over to her. The roses at the centre of the table were red and radiant.

"You know what – I am feeling hungry now, after smelling so much food which I am sure will be as tasty as it smells." And she was honest; the scent of freshly backed garlic bread and aroma of curry etc. was mouth-watering. Joe opened the oven door and took out the plate of garlic bread.

After a while, they sat down and a sumptuous dinner was served. Delicious crisp salad and wild rice with chicken curry in sherry sauce was not something Shirley had expected from a bachelor.

"Doctor, you are a good cook."

"Well, thank you, but I am not a doctor yet."

"May be you are not now, but I'm sure you would be a good doctor too."

"Well, I hope so. So tell me - have you always wanted to study medicine?"

"No. Not at all. In fact I was very scared when I had to dissect a frog, the first time. It was very slimy and sticky and all, and I used to ask everyone, why frog? Well, somebody told me that frogs and humans are vertebrates and they have similar organ systems etc. etc. but my question remained same – why bloody frogs? But when I grew up I knew I wanted to become a doctor because that was something I was passionate about; I wanted to spend time with people, an honest time in an honest environment, where I have time to listen to them and share their sufferings, and their pleasure on the road to recovery. Anyway, what about you, you always wanted to become a Doc?"

"Yes and I think for the same reason, probably I will repeat your words if I have to tell you."

"Well, hmm, I am pleased that we share the same feeling."

They finished the dinner in an hour and spent another hour on dinner table talking to each other and then came back to the living room with glasses of wine.

They shared the silence for few minutes. Joy was surprised that talking on phone was so easy for him but now only her presence was enough to make him feel captivated, he had never felt anything like that; her presence was giving him a sense of fulfilment. Was he already in love with her? He couldn't say but he knew only one thing that he wanted to be in love. It had been over a year since his last break up, but he had not been interested in anyone for a casual relationship. He knew, he could not find love but love had to find him and he had waited for that to happen, until he met Shirley. She was the one for whom he had felt so strongly. He wanted to be mad in love because that was the ultimate sanity to be achieved. He was ready to lose the joy of any materialistic thing he could ever wish, by only gaining the contentment of love. He sensed positive vibes coming from her, and somehow he felt that she was the one he was looking for.

"Have you ever been in love?" he found himself asking. He didn't feel embarrass.

This was his heart - not mind- talking. A mind was no use in matters of love. The ambience of serenity engulfed them. He waited to hear her.

"Being in love is a relative term, I suppose," she looked down and continued as if talking to herself, "If you love somebody for one and only reason and expectation – love - that is some form of love and if you get the same love in return, that is the only final form of love. Anything less, anything more will impure it," she paused for a moment and closed her eyes, "Yes, I am in love......with the 'love' I have to give it to such a person whom I can love with such purity."

He heard her hoarse voice.

He wanted to say and ask so many things but instead he said, "What is love?"

"If I say, love is a blissful insanity, love is trust, love is happiness, and I can go on and on, but a sane mind won't understand the sanity of love. A sane mind cannot feel the beauty and happiness of love. May be that's why, they say, love is a state of madness; it cannot be understood without being in that state." She expressed herself, slowly.

"If I say I am sensing that state?"

"What do you feel?"

"Delight of the heart."

"And?"

"Enchantment of the soul."

"And?"

"The oneness between us, that you can truly understand the words, without them ever being uttered. And I am feeling that highest sense of fulfilment."

"Then it makes two of us."

"Yes."

"And how long this feeling would last?"

"All my life, I have waited for this feeling and all you need to do is to hold my hand and we'll go forever. May be, I have kept this feeling out of sight till now, but then I never met anyone like you. I knew I cannot find someone to 'love' because 'love' has to be within ourselves and one has to be very lucky to have found it, and that is what I feel now – very lucky."

She held his hand on the table. He felt the warmth of her hand, of her trust, of her love. He had to put his hand on her hand, to give the same warmth, trust and love in return, because that was the only absolute trade for which he had waited for so long.

The emotional energy flowing between them had enthralled them in a state of mind where their world had shrunk to each other.

She wanted to say that I am ready to stay with you today, tomorrow and forever and that, yes, nothing matters now as long as I have you and the knowledge of your love; that I am unable to feel pain, sorrow or regret, from anything and anyone in the world, because I am in the ultimate state of happiness; of joy; of thankfulness."

Instead she said, "I think I should leave now."

"Can't you stay a bit long?"

"Yes…yes, I suppose I can."

Sensual pleasures were passing in the twinkling of an eye. They held their faces close to each other, as if they were waiting for their sensual pleasures to explode, and unite it together. They didn't touch each other but walked together towards the bedroom.

They un-tied their shoes and lay down on the bed, facing each other. After staring a couple of minutes, they simultaneously came closer to each other. They could feel the warmth of their trust; of their breaths; of their happiness; of their union. Their feet touched each other and a sense of unison exploded into each other, as if two electrical wires of different nodes had touched together and sparked. They brought their lips closer and touched slightly; only slightly. Their lips moved away and then came closer again to taste each other; this time for a bit long and then moved away again. They exchanged the taste of the saliva and they were desperate to taste it again. But they held it back, as if, it was too precious of a moment to touch it again, to dissipate it or to feel it. As if, the pleasure of the moment was increasing exponentially and it was worth waiting a bit longer. Only a bit longer.

He kissed her again and again on a varying speed, a bit harder, then softly and softly again. He placed his hand on her back and untied the lace of her dress. The beautiful maroon brassiere exposed her breasts through the net and his hand inevitably moved to stroke them gently. She felt a tremor exploded through her body. She slipped her hand on his belly and rolled his t-shirt up to his chest and kissed. Then he freed her finest pair, from the piece of cloth, and started discovering the finer curves of her body.

They continued exploring each other with a sense of urgency and a sense of preserveness, until they melted into each other, and their bodies, minds and souls became unified, and reached the highest state of tranquillity.

5. Disappearance

Joe woke up early in the morning with a sense of excitement. The small calendar on the bedside table was showing the date as 14th February. Of 'course it's Valentine's Day. It's going to be a very special day of my life. He muttered.

He had asked Shirley to come over his place. It was a special place for them where they have met first time after being in love and it was their second Valentine they were going to celebrate together. They both were then in their last year of medical term. Time had flown and so had their love to newer heights in the past two years.

"Joe! What you are up to, so early? Reeve shouted from the next bedroom, surprised to hear the noise from Joe's room.

"Nothing much. You can't help in this mate! It's not something you would be interesting in", he walked down to his room to have a morning chit-chat with Reeve.

"I know" he paused and then continued, "I know. Is Shirley coming over here today?"

"Yes, and as last year we would be going out for dinner tonight. Would you like to grace us with your presence, sir?" Joe chuckled.

"Not really, it would be too small of an event to grace it with my presence. Do enjoy yourself! But yes, maybe I can help you by not intruding you while you're here." Reeve replied.

Last year on Valentine's Day, Joe and Shirley had insisted Reeve to join on dinner. It was not as if they were merely trying to give him a company but it was because they liked his company. Reeve seemed as happy as anybody else without any relationship. It was as if relationship was a saddle for him. As if, why he would need a company when even without that he never shown a slightest hint of dreariness, resentment or remorse for anything or anybody in the world and yet there was an aura around him which smelled and asked for solitude. He was a world in himself, who was neither concerned for anybody, nor thwarted by anybody around him. Though, Joe and Shirley considered him as a brother, for Shirley he was an enigma. "In fact, he is kinda cute!" she had once told Joe. But then girls have weird tastes. And yet they were never able to say what Reeve's perception was about them because emotions were one thing he was alien with. That night, last year, their dinner party was quite funny and may be embarrassing for them. After the meal, they had ordered drinks but as usual Reeve had opted not to have any drink so that he can drive them back home. After a few drinks, Shirley had got in a bit of mood and asked Joe if he could dance with her and Reeve had answered for him, "Of course he would, he would do anything for you.", Reeve pumped him up, knowing well that he could barely walk at that time. It would have been only wise for Joe to turn down the offer but instead he went ahead and asked her, "Which dance would you like?"

"Tangoooooo!!" She cried in excitement.

When they started dancing, they moved so fast that others started clearing the floor for them and after a couple of minutes, they were the centre of attention and everybody in the room was watching them. But then came the moment when they both fell flat on the floor in each other's arms. In an instant they came back in their senses and realized everybody was watching them but their embarrassment was instantly vanished when they realized the humour of the moment, Joe kissed her passionately while flat on the floor before they got up and everybody clapped and appreciated the unexpected fun. On the way home, they made joke about who stepped over whom and made them fell.

Clock's hands moved to show the time as 10.30 AM and it was another half an hour for Shirley to come. He had completed most of the cooking himself though Shirley had asked him to wait for her so that they could cook together but he was just eager to make her feel very special today, as it was going to be a special day for them. Reeve had left the house at around 9 am with his painting stuff which he took with him often when he left for some unknown place that he never bothered to tell Joe, despite being asked several times.

He had prepared the same dishes which he cooked when Shirley came at his place for the first time and even decided to wear the same clothes which they wore when they met first time in this house, and luckily the clothes were still in good condition.

At exactly 11.05 am there was a knock on the door. Joe peeped through the window and unlocked the door, he hid his face behind the lavish bouquet of red roses and they both chorused, "Happy Valentine's day", he moved away the bouquet from his face and saw that Shirley was also moving away the bouquet away from her face simultaneously, it was as if he was seeing in a mirror. And perhaps, they were mirror image of each other in every sense one would perceive necessary for happiness. The trust they had between themselves was as if, they have known each other, since eternity, yet, the freshness and fragrance of their love was as if, they have just discovered each other.

Joe placed his hands on her back and started kissing her. Then they moved towards couch vehemently while holding each other. They caressed each other for some time and then stopped and held back their desires - but excited in anticipation.

"I have a little gift for you", she said and took out a packet from her bag.

He took the packet and removed the packaging. It was a book and the title read 'The Saviour – Never lets her go'.

"Wow! Great! You are ever so thoughtful". This was the book which he randomly mentioned to Shirley long back that he was not finding in the stores and though he had read it, he wanted to keep it in his collection.

"And as you might expect I have a gift, rather two gifts for you", he said excitedly, though, with a hint of nervousness.

He walked to the wall side cabinet and took out the packets. He handed over a packet to Shirley and said, "Here you go!"

She opened it up and found several hardboard pieces in different shapes, she looked puzzled.

"It's a puzzle and you can try and solve it now", he suggested.

"Sure." She took the challenge. It looked like pieces of some beautiful scenery but there were several letters on all over the places which were in foreign languages, unknown to her.

She started putting together pieces by concentrating on the scenery. After she joined few pieces a line appeared over the scenery as:

Italian: " lo sposerete?"

And when she joined few more pieces another line appeared over the scenery.

Portuguese: "Queres casar comigo?"

And then,

Japanese: "watashito kekkon shite kuremasuka?"

And then,

Finnish: "Haluatko naida minut?"

And then,

French: "Veux-tu m'épouser?"

And then,

German: "Willst Du mich heiraten?"

And all the pieces were joined together and puzzle was complete then. But Shirley still looked bewildered as the words on the scenery were no good to her.

"If any of these lines is no good to you then you may want to turn over this board and see it's back", Joe advised her.

She turned back and realized that, in the grey background, some words in red were appeared diagonal to the board.

The words read: WILL YOU MARRY ME?

She was astonished, but didn't say a word, as if, the silence was enough to grasp the moment, as if no words were enough to say anything.

He gave another small box to her and said, "But second part of this puzzle is yet to be completed."

She quickly unpacked in anticipation and found that it was a gold locket with a heart shape pendant. "It's beautiful!" She was elated.

"But you have to solve it yet."

She looked closely and opens the pendant in two halves. One half had a small picture of Joe and other half had a picture of Shirley and the pendant was so big that it has a beautiful ring inside.

He got down on one knee and asked her, "Will you marry me?"

She waited for a moment, perplexed, as if, she was not prepared for the moment, OR, as if it was obligatory to offer few moments before burdening with what was needed to say.

"I love you and I always will. A marriage is unjust without love; a marriage is a betrayal without love. But a love is neither unjust nor betrayal without marriage. And I love you and I always will. But in a marriage, I have to make some commitments; commitment to make our life happy and satisfied; commitment to help you and be with you when you chase your and our dreams; commitment to make you feel special in the same way as you will to me; commitment to be truthful and be able to gain your trust and confidence. And I don't think I am ready for this. For this reason I must not accept this.

I am indebted to you for asking me to marry you but I am equally hurtful for the pain my words may cause to you".

She left the house without staying any further. He was devastated on what had happened. He would have been less shocked if he would have least imagined the outcome but then he had to accept it as it was. He had pursued her all that afternoon to tell the reason why she wasn't ready for this yet, but all she had said, "I'm just not ready for this", and he had to accept that. He felt as if she was either trying to hide something or wanted to tell something but couldn't decide. She looked pale and worn out in trying to struggle against her wish.

In the past few months, a void had developed in their relationship which was strange, at times disturbing, and beyond any reasoning for Joe. No, maybe I am just imagining things, he had thought many times. But that day he was sure that something had either changed or was changing her and the mere thought of being without her was destroying him. But there were no easy answers as to why she had been denying meeting him frequently. And even from some time she had stopped staying overnight with him completely.

"I am too busy these days in my project; I have to go early in the morning to attend an important lecture. My mother is coming over to meet me so we can't meet." The excuses were feeble and repetitive.

One afternoon, he waited over an hour in a fine restaurant over a dinner date for her to arrive and when she came, she wanted to leave without even having food. That was not the first and last time she had made him wait and been unable to come. She had lost her mobile few months back and after a few days, Joe had asked her, "Hey, why are you not getting yourself a new mobile? I can't talk to you when I want and it just makes me miserable." And when she didn't reply, he added, "OK, just leave it - I'll get a new mobile for you when I see you next time."

"No, please you don't worry. I think I will take some time off from mobile. Beside, when I am at Uni, I will be busy and won't be able to talk you anyway and at home you can call me on my landline", Shirley had defended. He remotely wondered whether her mobile was really lost or she had just lied about it.

Sometimes his calls were not answered when he called up on her landline but he had a feeling that she was there, just near the phone and yet didn't pick it up, and yet he hated to accept that she was avoiding him. And sometimes when she picked the phone, her answers were not so sweet but short.

"What you were doing?"

"Nothin n you."

"I was remembering you."

"Kkk"

Hey, why are you so silent?"

"Am not."

"Can you meet me tomorrow?"

"Nah"

And he would have to say 'bye' after a couple of minutes, thinking maybe it was not really the best of time to call her. Once they had decided to go to a nearby beach and Shirley was not even interested to take a walk and he remembered, how their earlier trips have had been full of life and joy when they had walked along the beach, holding each other's hand or ran into the water to play with the mild waves coming to the shore. It had been fifteen days, since he last met her on Valentine's Day. She was not picking the phone and then he had called at her parent's place. Her mother Kate had picked the phone.

"Hi Kate, umm, actually I was trying to contact Shirley but seems she is not there. I thought, maybe you will know where she is." Joe enquired.

"No, I'm afraid I have no idea where she is, but do let me know as well when you get to know about her", Kate had lied.

Shirley was with her at that very moment and had asked Kate to lie. "You should not be doing this to Joe; I think you are making a mistake. You must talk to him and tell him everything", Kate had advised Shirley after she finished with Joe.

After that Joe had called at the medical college and found out that she was not going there for a week. And the same day he had received a post. It was a short letter from Shirley.

"Dear Joe,

I know you must be looking for me; you must be angry with me and you must be worried about me. And for that reason I have to write you to tell that I am leaving on a new journey, a new life, a new space and a new set of people around me. Please, you must not try to contact me. I wish you know, how much I am conscious of the suffering this will cause upon you. And, how unlucky I am that I have to ask you for your forgiveness not only for what I'm doing but also for not being able to give you the reasons for doing this. I won't give you my reasons for doing this because a reason can be fought with a reason and yet either reason can be sacred. But, I hope, if I give you the knowledge of the fact that there is nothing you could have done to prevent me doing this, it may lessen your interest to know my reasons. You must have to remember always that it is me who is at fault and who don't think, can do justice with you and your love. Try not to hurt yourself too much.

41

I must say goodbye now and ask you to leave me and my memories, to have yourself a wonderful life waiting for you. Love, Shirley".

He later found out that she had left the medicine, when she was just four months away to complete it, to become a doctor. He contacted her parents but they couldn't tell him where she had gone. He contacted everybody she knew but nobody could tell him, where she was.

Shirley was gone.

6. A Family

Reeve felt exhausted and swam to the bank, cutting the waves from his long hands like a knife. He climbed to the highest landscape and sat naked at the face of the rock. The downhill sun was glowing on his wet body. The river waves below him were coming to the shore to touch the stones and were playing the music of its own. The rock, he was sitting on, was complimenting the long and rugged curves of his body. The water droplets on his body were shining like crystals by reflecting sunshine. The combination of his body and droplets were looking, as if, lava had erupted from the belly of the earth and was drying up to form the rock. It was his sanctuary and a place to rejuvenate himself. It was an isolated, undisturbed and untamed place but everything he needed. There were mild waves of the river to fight with him and contain his anger when he swam. There were rocks to give him rest and there were winds to cool him down. There were birds to talk to him and there were lush green trees to rejuvenate his spirits and energy. All he missed was the suffering of the world; the prejudices of the people; the vulnerability of his own character; the pain of the emotions; the violence of the cowards; the evil of the sanctions; the impurity of the thoughts; the inability to trust. This was a place for his self-realization and he was frequently drawn towards it. It was his world, full of everything he liked.

Thirty years back, when a little boy was born in Harvey's family, Mr. Harvey was the happiest man. This was his first child and a son. He always wished that he had a son so when he grew up he would enjoy playing football, cricket, video games etc. and do all sort of stuff boys do. Though they were offered to know the sex of the baby after Jane had her second ultrasound but they both denied as it was their first child and they wanted to keep the suspense alive. But it was Jane who wished for a daughter, as her first child. 'It's my sweet little girl and I think we should buy all the baby stuff for a girl', Jane would say laying a hand on her unborn baby. 'No, no. It's my boy! You see, he had already started playing football in your tummy', William would reply touching his wife's belly. After quite a few funny arguments, they had agreed to prepare a 'baby room' with the colours and stuff which would complement both, a baby boy or a girl, but they also continued, shopping specific to their own beliefs. 'Oh! This Barbie doll is a must for my baby', Jane said once, while shopping. 'You go on for this and I will find something good for my boy', William had chuckled. It was after ten hours of hard labour when finally William saw his baby and he was ecstatic. He kissed his wife, baby and midwives and cried with joy and excitement. He was over the moon and felt a sense of accomplishment - it was his own creation; a part of him. He called his family and friends to give them the big news. Jane was equally delighted; she held the baby in her arms, crying, and thought it was all worth – the intolerable and long bouts of pain. William had thrown a big celebration party at London's top Club, Marksmen and all their family, friends and colleagues were invited. Jane was a bit disappointed to see that nobody except her couple of friends and colleagues had turned up in the party and the flood of Williams's colleagues and friends had only seemed to have added more twinge in her heart. In the past two months of her pregnancy leave, her company seemed to had forgotten her. Nobody had made any contact with her. She was a 'Designer' with a prestigious corporate communication consultancy firm who worked across identity and brochures in the construction, financial, banking and private investment markets. William was a 'Finance controller' with a leading multi-billion pound construction company with offices all around the world and UK. He was only thirty two and it was a fantastic achievement for his age. They both had moved up the corporate ladder hard way but quickly. They both worked hard and studied part time, while doing their full time job and that was the reason they didn't have any time for a serious relationship until they had met each other. They both had the same enthusiasm and energy, and may be these were the similarities which brought them together when they first met during a presentation conducted by Jane for advertisement of a new mega shopping mall being constructed by William's company. "I think this ad will surely boost this project and I hope everybody else like it as well." William had said after the presentation.

"And so do I, by the way, if this round of presentation goes well, our company have planned a dinner party this Friday to discuss it further", Jane said.

"I am sure we will meet at dinner", William said smiling. And when they met at dinner, they were instantly charmed by each other. Their physical attributes complemented each other – she was almost six feet, sharp featured, with hazel green eyes and a figure suited for a mannequin dressed in a designer's showroom. She wore glasses but they only seemed to have added more elegance to her beauty, and when she spoke everybody listened, as if she had cast a spell on them. He was six feet two inch tall, lean with long muscular arms and a face who wore a maturity that made him look wise, beyond his years.

"I take that you are single", William said with confidence.

"You reckon", Jane said smilingly.

"I am thinking to drive down to lakes this weekend, would you care to come?" William asked.

"I think I can make it but on one condition", Jane replied.

"And what is that?"

"If I am the only one, you are dating with", Jane said smilingly.

"Hahaha! You bet, I am", he laughed aloud.

They both knew that they were drawn to each other naturally. Only after six weeks of dating each other, William had proposed her for marriage, while sailing through the Europe, on the deck of Queen Mary 2. It was a beautiful full moon night. By the time they were married, Jane was carrying William's child. They christened the boy as Reeve. It was an exciting and tough time for the first time parents. Jane still had four months pregnancy leave left, but at times she wanted to run away from the house and the child. She felt utter monotony in her life. Perhaps, it had something to do with post pregnancy baby blues.

She woke up in the nights to feed her baby so couldn't sleep much and days were full of chores, and yet she felt bored and trapped in the house. She felt guilty that she was not enjoying the moments with her own baby. She could not understand what that was. Before William was back to his office after two weeks of parenting leave, they seemed to have enjoyed their time together with the baby. But now Jane was on her own with the baby. She missed the energy and excitement of boardrooms meetings. She missed corporate luncheons and dinners and the exciting presentations she gave. She missed the times when everyone listened, spelled by her wit and charm. She missed having a laugh with her colleagues at the coffee machine and their little chit-chat. Her whole world seemed to had changed completely in the last few months, and to add to her frustration William had been too busy lately. After his last promotion, he had to tour frequently all over the UK and abroad to attend various important meetings. Staying back late in the evenings was like a part of the prestigious post he held in his company. She thought, having a baby should have been so pleasant and enjoyable time but why the things seem to have turned upside down. Perhaps things are not so bad; perhaps I am just a little depressed or maybe it's merely baby blues, and probably I should see a psychiatrist. She couldn't decide.

"How you both are doing? Is Reeve managing to keep you on edge?" William said that night when he returned from office.

"We are good, but this is not funny. I am sick of staying at home. I want to cancel my leaves and return to job."

"And who do you think is going to look after Reeve? I don't want to see him in nursery, not yet."

"Then maybe you can take a few weeks holidays – you can still apply for parental leaves, can't you?"

"That's out of question. It's a very busy time. I would rather resign but talking about leave is a definite 'no'."

When Reeve was barely four months old, Janet returned on her job and Reeve was in a day care nursery. Though, going back to work meant a very busy life for her but she was ambitious and was delighted to be back, and it took her some time to regain her edge but her chief was only too happy to see her since her sheer enthusiasm and determination was exemplary. Though, her excitement was short lived - for good or bad. That day when she was in the middle of a meeting with her team to discuss an ad campaign she was working on, she felt uneasy and sick and had rushed to toilets. She had not even taken her lunch yet and had a light breakfast that morning. She could not understand why she got sick. *It must be just a bug,* she thought.

Next evening when she was about to take dinner with William, she was sick again.

"Did you eat something which you think might be the reason?" William asked Janet.

"No! Nothing. As a matter of fact this is the second time since yesterday that I am sick."

"Do you think you need a pregnancy test?"

"No, I won't like to think so, but it may be a possibility?"

That night Janet could not sleep, she was not enthusiastic at all on the thought of being pregnant again that soon. Next day before going to office, she went to a nearby pharmacy and brought a home pregnancy test kit. She waited eagerly for the result, it was a 'plus' sign. She felt desperate and took the test again. It was not going to change though.

"Bill, I am pregnant – I took a test in the morning", she informed when they met in evening.

"Really, that's a great news. You should have informed me, as soon as you knew."

"I wanted to talk about this. I think I am not ready for this yet. Reeve is too young."

"What has that to do with this, he is in the day care anyway."

"Well, yeah. But maybe one child is enough for us. These days bringing up even one child is not easy, and if we can care for one properly, that is good enough."

"Yeah, maybe you are right. But Reeve needs some company, we have to think about him first."

"Well maybe after some time, but I am not mentally and physically prepared for it now."

"Well, I can certainly say you are a very strong woman but if you are not ready for this yet then darling, maybe you will be, in due course", William tried to ease her.

"And what about my career? Last time I missed a promotion because of the pregnancy and it may happen again."

"Well, in that case you may want to sue your company for harassment", William chuckled.

"Bill! I am not kidding, I am dead serious."

"Yeah, me too. Don't worry about that, you don't have to take long holidays this time."

"And what exactly you have in mind?"

"You will know."

But a little surprise was yet to come before them. When they visited the surgery for her ultrasound, they were amazed to see the little screen – they were going to have twins.

When Reeve was exactly one year and seventy days old, three days before Christmas, Jane gave birth to Jim and Jessica. It was a perfect Christmas for them. Celebration was in the air. Janet had told little Reeve that Santa had brought this year not one but two gifts for all of us. William was thrilled to see his three children, he had arranged their beds in a row and one night he called Janet in kid's room and said, "Look at them, how beautiful they all are looking, sleeping in a row, next to each other."

"Yes, it's so lovely, isn'it."

After the Christmas holidays, when William went to office, he returned early.

"You are so early today? Jane asked inquisitively.

"Yes, and I don't need to go anymore."

"What!!"

"I have resigned."

It was not an easy decision for him to leave an extremely well paid job but then he had to choose, and he chose more important things in life. He thought, spending time with kids was far better investment than earning those bucks. "Yes, that is what matters most to me, giving a better start to my kids." He enjoyed his new routine and role and cared for them as much as he could and only when they all started going to nursery; he took a part time job as an accountant in a company. He was then going twice a week for full days. But perhaps his kids needed more than that; they needed their mother who was busier than ever in her job and was frequently out on the company tour for days and weeks. They needed their mother not for hugs, they expected when they came home tired; not for her hand made pies and cakes when they were so hungry; not for reading them a story or a song from a nice kiddie's book; not for a walk to the nearest park; not for answering all the inquisitive & exhaustive questions, they had all day long; and not for all the emotional support they needed; but for that she would have seen the troubled relationship which was slowly and innocently brewing up between the siblings. Reeve was now five years old and being the eldest came with added expectation of being better; expectation of being more understanding and behaving more maturely with his siblings. It was as if, he had to grow up faster than he needed to. After Jim and Jessica were born, his life was suddenly changed. A child of his age, who depended on his mother for all his physical and emotional sustenance, barely got any company from his mother or from his father. Janet was never at home and William was busy coping with the twin's needs most of the time, and nobody could blame him for focusing his attention on them – caring for the two new born babies could have been difficult even for their mother and without even William realizing Reeve got pushed away to the side. Reeve was now five years of age; it was an age when he needed a lot of attention and direction to shape up his character and future, yet, he didn't get all the attention he wanted. He missed his mom; he waited for the evenings when she would come back and hug him. She is the only one who loves me, no one else is good enough, he thought.

He was becoming a very aggressive child. At the age of seven he was suspended from the school when he viciously attacked his classmate, with his sharpened pencil. The boy had asked Reeve, after seeing his belt missing a couple of loops on his waist, "Why your mother can't even dress you properly?" His teacher had later explained to William, "Reeve's behaviour is extremely offensive to everyone in the class including teachers and he doesn't concentrate on things taught to him; he is the rudest child in the class. He is not sociable at all. I don't know why he is like that but I am sure Mr. Harvey, you will be able to understand him and will take good care of him". And when William came home after meeting his teacher, he took good care of him - he slapped him hard and yelled, "You made me ashamed. You are no good. See your brother and sister; they are a year younger than you but more intelligent and mannered. They are winning prizes over prizes and here you are? You can't even write a word correctly. This is all because your mother loves you so much."

Reeve didn't speak a word. He wanted to crawl under a rock and hide. He hated it; he hated it more because he had to face this all in front of Jim and Jessica. This was not the first time but the relentless criticism he has to bear these days, mostly from his father. It was not the kind of comparison parents do to inspire their children but the one, which was full of loathing and yet blatantly favourable towards the twins and which could only throw him down the abyss of bitterness and confusion, and which was knocking his confidence right down to the bottom. There were no dearth of reasons to scold him; it was either, when he had done something wrong or else when Jim and Jessica had done something good; either way he was below par than twins and for them they lived, as if, Reeve never existed. One day, when Jim and Jessica were playing the role of doctor and patient, Reeve came and said, "I also want to play with you."

"No", they both shouted together, "Let us finish the game, you go away", Jim added.

Reeve pulled out the cloth on which they had set up there little hospital and threw away all the stuff. It didn't help him; William locked him up in a room for a couple of hours as a punishment and he was even more lonelier now. They both were a team; together in everything, up against him. They were the most obeying and good mannered children in front of Mr. & Mrs Harvey's, but behind their back they were scheming against Reeve to seclude him from everything and everywhere. How could their parents believe Reeve for anything against twins, as for them they were the perfect ones? Perhaps, the hardest times for Reeve were when even his mother, Janet, took the side of twins and disapproved him outright. Once, when Janet had praised Jim for his good drawing work and asked Reeve to take some inspiration from him, it was too much of an inspiration for Reeve. He got up in the middle of the night, when everybody was asleep, went to the study room and tore apart Jim's drawing book in small pieces, put in a plastic bag and threw it in a bin. Whereabouts of Jim's drawing book, remained a mystery but the twins always suspected that it had to do with Reeve.

They were learning things faster and together while Reeve was having difficulty to concentrate. He was careless and withdrawn from most of the things. He was then twelve and was regularly getting bad marks in school. His teacher had met William again to discuss him and said, "Mr. William, I think, may be you need to spend more time with him. He needs more participation, more care and encouragement". But that didn't change a thing. When William and Janet were not around, the twins took decision for him, they told him what to do and what not to do. William and Jane unintentionally allowed many things to Jim and Jessica whereas forbidden to Reeve. When a pop band came to the city, Jim & Jessica were going with their friends with consent of William and when Reeve told Janet at the dinner table that he also wanted to go, Jessica jumped in the conversation and said, "There will be a mad rush in this event, beside you are not a big fan of them and if you really want to listen, I'll get you a CD." They all agreed on this. Reeve was silent, he neither denied, nor agreed.

7. Transformation

There were only three days left in 14th July to celebrate Jane's birthday. Jessica & Jim had planned to give a surprise party at Jessica's friend Amy. Mrs. Ann Robinson had loved the idea as both, the daughters and mums were good friends.

"I think our back garden has sufficient space for a small barbeque party". Mrs. Robinson suggested.

"Yes, we will invite very few people who are close to mum and us". Jessica agreed.

"And I have checked the weather forecast on couple of weather sites and this whole week is going to be very sunny", Jim had said.

"You don't really believe in forecasts; do you, especially for typical British weather?" Amy chuckled.

"Not really, but at least in a month like July, forecast of a nice weather is not too risky to take, moreover in last two years I remember, weather on mum's birthday had been very nice. Do you remember Jessica, last year we went to Blackpool to celebrate and the weather was so nice?" Jim convinced.

"Yes, that is right." Jessica replied.

"Where is Reeve, does he know about all this?" Mrs. Robinson asked.

"We will tell him, once we have planned everything." Jessica replied.

"Or may be, we will give him a surprise too", Jim joked.

"Hahaha," Amy laughed on his joke.

"It's your elder brother we are talking - he would want to be a part of this surprise, as much as you both; don't you think so? Mrs. Robinson gave a frown to Jessica and Jim.

A day before her birthday, Janet asked William to come with her for a long drive in a country side. They both liked to go for long drives. It was a fine whether. The engine of her convertible roared with life as she turned the key into slot. Soon, she was running on the highways, crossing the national speed limit. "So it's your 45th birthday tomorrow – any special wish?" William had asked Janet when they reached on a long highway.

"Um! OK, let me think", she replied.

"Before that you need to take your foot off the gas pedal, you're already running at 110 miles", William said with a hint of stressed lines on his forehead.

She ignored the warning, "This birthday, I want to dance with you", she said gaily.

At that moment, car suddenly jerked and rocketed towards the concrete divider on their right side. Car's right tyre was blown and she had lost control of the car. Car had hit the concrete divider and spun out of control.

William was in coma for two days and when he woke up, he saw his three children beside him, "Where is Janet?" he shouted. Children ran to call the doctor.

"Where is Janet" he shouted again.

Doctor and nurses tried to calm him, "Mr. Harvey you are not in a position to talk about anything".

Reeve didn't know how he had to react to the news. He had waited in the evenings to meet his mother, to hug her, to tell her things which he could not say to anybody, to hear that she loved him, to do things together. It was beyond his comprehension that she would never be there to come again and hug him. His mind wanted to explode but he couldn't cry. He couldn't cry in the day because the loss for him was too sacred to share with someone but when everyone was asleep he cried alone, all the night till dawn, for days, weeks and months. William's both the knee caps were damaged and he was on a wheelchair. In a spur of moment all was changed, all was gone. Those days everybody behaved weirdly and at their free will. For days, weeks and months there were neither any suggestion nor guidance offered by William, nor any kind of restraining from him for his kids. It was like everyone was in their own world - lost and careless. They ate, slept and did whatever they wanted to do at different times and in different ways. Reeve tried on a class-A drug and found it the easiest way to escape from everything.

One day when he was taking drugs with his neighbour Tom in his back garden, Tom's father Dan came in to see them and was shocked to realize, what he saw, though, he pretended that he had not seen and understood what was happening. He was sure of only one thing that his son had no reason to go for drugs. He must have been dragged into trying that, he thought. I don't have to worry about Tom, all I have to do is to is transform his mislaid source – Reeve. And he was quite confident to be able to help him. Mr. Dan Mosley was a child psychiatrist.

When Reeve was gone, he called upon his son and said, "My dear dear son! Can I ask you a favour please?"

Tom came to him and he lowered his eyes and replied, "Dad, I know you have seen us. Are you angry with me? I am sorry."

"No, I am not angry with you. But I want you to help your friend Reeve. Will you do that for me please?"

After a long conversation with his son, he dialled William's phone number and said, "Bill, I met Reeve today and he looks pretty lost in some way but he enjoyed time with Tom…can you try to make him come to play with Tom regularly".

"I am really glad to hear that he enjoys his time with Tom, in fact he has been quite aloof and quiet for some time and it will be really good for him to have a company. Thanks Dan", William said. After that day Dan was always with them watching, participating and supporting them when they played and studied together. Dan was 45, but he looked young and full of energy. His long curly blonde hair bounced around his neck when he played football with them. He told them jokes, stories and shared his life experiences, and boys just loved him. When he was with them, he was into their world; he was silly, played along, had fun and behaved like one of them and yet, he was supporting and guiding them as an adult. They were spending more and more time together.

After a couple of weeks Dan went to see William and said, "I would like to know something about Reeve but before that I want to tell you something. I think Reeve is having some problem which we call in medical term as Learning Disability and it is because he is suffering from a kind of psychiatric condition. I don't want to frighten you but I think you can help him if I tell you that he was taking drugs until a few days back."

William was shaken to hear all the things Dan told him but he believed him because he had seen all the symptoms Dan described him. He felt guilty for Reeve's condition. He asked Dan to help him as a psychiatrist and told him what he wanted to know about Reeve. Dan also helped him in understanding Reeve's condition and told him, how he can work effectively with Reeve.

After he got William's consent, he had more time to spend with Reeve and cure him; but Reeve was more than a patient to him; he had seen him growing up as a child and to put him on to the right path meant a lot to him. In last few weeks, he had done a comprehensive evaluation of Reeve's condition and he had to work on the several components. Dan had formed a very special bond with Reeve in the last few weeks. It was something Reeve was missing in his life. Somebody who could listen to him, understand him and guide him. Reeve had then started coming around more often and opened up to Dan. Dan was learning different things about Reeve from the way he acted, the way he ate, even the way he wrote and walked. They talked in great lengths on various issues and each time Reeve appeared more calm and understanding than ever before.

"What are your goals in life, do you know what you want to become when you're grown up?"

"I never thought of this. There is nothing great in my life to think. Nobody ever loved me, perhaps my mother loved me, but even she left me."

"Do you love yourself?"

"Myself? I guess not really, why?"

"Well, there you go. If you can't love yourself then how can you expect or even blame somebody not to love yourself. First learn to love yourself by virtue of your own actions and beyond that nothing matters. If you are taking drugs, doing things which are wrong for you and people around you; and hating others that make you guilty in your own eyes, you will never be able to love yourself. Until then nothing can help you."

"Nobody helps me anyway except you. Tim, my best friend in school, now is on Henry's side who bullies me always. Paul has stopped talking to me suddenly without giving me any reason, though he always claimed that he was my best friend, a big liar - a friend never does anything like that. Even my brother and sister are always cross with me. They never share anything with me."

"You know Reeve everyone is unique and so are you. No matter what you do, there will be a uniqueness and sacredness about you which others won't have. People of this world doesn't matter more than yourself, and you are worrying and wasting your own life for them. If you look around, there are so many things and events which you'll find appalling but the truth is that your heart will hold hate and anger against them but you won't be able to change them. And when you hate them, you try to resist them or show your anger to them, at that moment, you submit to them. You submit your inner self to them, your morality, your existence, your beliefs and your uniqueness & sacredness. At that moment you become one of them. At that moment you live in THEIR world."

He leaned towards Reeve and continued, "The key is - detach them, ignore them, don't feel them, don't let them touch your sacredness. Don't resist them. Let them co-exist. Have you ever seen a sandal wood tree? I guess no, let me tell you. On a sandal tree in a forest, hundreds of poisonous snakes may be wrapped around but it doesn't stops producing its scent because it doesn't know, doesn't feel their existence, but they co-exist. Nothing and nobody, but YOU make your own world. You have to create a shield to guard your own existence, your own world, your inner self, your beliefs and your sacredness, from those who want to destroy it and whom you want to hate. You and only you are responsible for your own actions and you cannot, ever, put onus on to somebody for what you become or what you are or what you make out of yourself. Don't seek for friendliness. Don't look for compassion or sympathy. Don't keep any expectation and don't expect any favours. You are your own greatest friend. There is nothing more sacred than loving yourself. Nobody, but you. You are the power! You are the world! You are the motion! You are the happiness! You are the greatest creation of all!"

That night Reeve could not sleep. Dan's words were echoing in his mind again and again and each time he felt as if those words gave him a kind of power and confidence he never had before. His whole life was reeling in his mind, he was trying to remember everything he hated or loved in his life and he was trying to relate those words with them. It was as if, he was weaving those words with all those events and it was taking his pain and anger away from it. He was changed forever.

One day when Reeve came to see Dan, he was painting in his garden and Reeve was mesmerized to see that beautiful painting and said, "When did you start painting, I never knew you can paint."

"Some things in life are only for you, you do them because you like doing that, you create them, you reflect your heart and soul, your inner self in doing that. Anyway, what is your passion in life?"

"Nobody ever made me realize that I am capable of anything, let alone a passion in my life. Though, I must not blame anybody for not doing the things in the way I could have done. And I must thank you to come in my life, like a guarding angel and enlightening my senses, my power and my world. I will always be indebted to you. But I think I like swimming." He concluded.

"They say, you should have at least two passions in your life, one for your body and one for you soul and mind. So if you like I can teach you paint as well?"

"Yes, sure. I think I would enjoy that."

He really enjoyed painting and it became one of his best pastimes. And whenever he felt low in spirits he had taken shelter of swimming and painting and it always worked for him.

8. A Horse Trainer

After a few days, Reeve joined 'Cornmil Primary Care Trust' and it was his first day in a hospital as a doctor. Senior Dr. Adrian Morris took him on a tour to show the hospital around and to meet and interact with his patients. Dr. Adrian was in his late 50s, a fat and huge guy with a wicked sense of humour and a goatee beard. It was time for Dr. Adrian's morning tour to his patients. He went room to room and bed to bed meeting with his patients. "You need to be patient as well before dealing with all of those here", he told Reeve.

"This is Martina. She has come for abdominal pain but GGT shows damaged hepatocytes due to excessive alcoholism are causing elevations in liver enzymes AST/ALT. So, next time a patient comes to you with abdominal pain you need to dig out how badly she or he has been enjoying life," Dr Adrian explained and moved to the next patient after a brief check-up and taking some notes.

"This is Tim. He was trying to impress his girlfriend in the kitchen when the hot oil in the pan caught fire and you can see the result." Tim had received third degree burns in upper half of his body.

After a while they entered in another room and Dr. Adrian whispered in Reeve's ear, "There she is, my favourite patient, but you need to be a bit careful – she will eat the bones out of you." He went near to her and said, "Meet Helen, Helen Caspero. Her dear horse had thrown her on the ground and she has a torn meniscus." The medial and lateral menisci (plural of meniscus) of the knee are two crescent bowl shaped disks of tough tissue that lie between the ends of the upper leg bone and lower leg bone that form the knee joint. She was a blue eyed brunette in her thirties with medium height. But she looked taller with her lean body and a lean face. She was sitting on her bed and reading a magazine, 'Racehorses'. She looked more like a prisoner than a patient on that bed. Later Dr. Adrian told Reeve that he had to pursue her a great deal to stay in the hospital for a while until she was fit enough to go. They then moved on to other patients and finished the morning round.

Later in the day Reeve was sent to make a round of the patients on his own and make a report. And when he came to Helen's bed, he enquired her, "Have you had all the medicines on time?"

"Of course I had. I am fit now and I want to leave this place NOW."

"But you can't walk yet, can you?"

"I still have one leg perfectly OK, so don't worry."

"I heard you are a horse trainer."

"I heard you are a doctor." She replied crisply.

"What kind of a horse trainer you are that you fell down from a horse?"

"Do you doctors supposed to treat all the illnesses in the world and never fail?" She looked straight in Reeve's eyes and replied.

"You look intelligent, though, you have a bull's attitude."

"And though you are trying to be confident, you look a novice here."

"Yes, indeed I am."

He consulted her file and some papers and said, "By seeing your X-ray report and everything, I think you can go by tomorrow. But I can't guarantee yet, I need to discuss this with Dr. Morris."

"Thanks." By seeing her facial expressions, it was difficult to say if she really meant it.

"No need to say thanks, you can repay me by allowing me to see your horses sometime"

"I don't think my horses will like you."

"But I can certainly say that one of your horse didn't like you either", he said pointing towards her injured leg.

"That was my own mistake."

"It's a nice start. At least you've started accepting things."

"Hey! Why I am here - to answer you OR to get treated?" She asked with a brisk tone.

"You are at the right place at the right time. I'll see what I can do." He said without seeing her face and moved away.

Next day Reeve came to see Helen and informed her that she was given the consent to be discharged from the hospital.

"Morning." He greeted her.

"Hey rookie!" She replied.

"I still want to see your horses." He said.

"But my horses need a vet, not you."

"Don't worry, they won't harm me."

"My address is in your files."

"I've noted already. I just needed your consent."

"You are very stubborn."

"Thank you for your compliment but I am just determined and straightforward."

After a few days, Joe also joined 'Eastbourne Surgery' to spend a year in general clinical training as PRHOs. Though, Joe had to drive over an hour to reach his hospital, he preferred to stay with Reeve so that he had a company when he came back in evenings. They shared their interesting highlights of the days with each other that most of the time was a good source of something to laugh about. They also shared their medical knowledge with each other that'd help them in their career.

Though, Reeve had taken Helen's farm address he didn't have any intention to go any time soon and after a few days he forgot about the conversation. One day when he was working on a painting at his usual isolated place, which was like a sanctuary for him, he remembered about the horses. It was six o'clock in the evening; he packed his painting gears and jumped into his car. He remembered the address; she had told him that it's in Osterley and it is the biggest farm near 'Lockheed pub' on the outskirts of London. It was not before 7 o'clock when he reached there.

It was a beautiful place in a quiet countryside area located on the hills with a panoramic view overseeing the mountains and a small river. The beautiful, well managed and neatly fenced meadows to form several grazing cells were being used by as much as twenty horses. It had shaded stables and another fenced area nearby, filled with barriers of structured wooden frames and bamboos, which looked like a loose jumping school for the horses. He was fascinated by the richness of that place. He looked around and asked a man about Helen, who was lean and young, possibly in his early thirties. The man pointed towards the far area where several horses were grazing. He recognized her though she was almost hidden amongst her horses. He walked down there and stopped. Looking from a short distance at her and her horses, as if it was natural for him to come here, as if an artist was inspecting his latest painting.

"Hey Rookie! Why have you have come here?" She asked, admiring and stroking the face of a horse. She didn't feel a need to look at him.

"To make some paintings."

"Do you really think I can possibly like you a bit?

"Absolutely not. I wouldn't have come here if I'd have thought so", he paused for a moment and continued, "I came here because I know you hate me and I can do some painting without you bothering me."

"Then go and do it, you're allowed."

He put his stuff on the grass outside of a grazing cell, unfolded his painting board and began painting. He painted for an hour and half and then left. Neither of them spoke.

He went there a few times after that, but they seldom spoke to each other. Later, he came to know that she was living there with her mother and three of her associates who lived nearby. Her mother, Mrs Judy Caspero, admired his paintings.

"Why don't you draw a painting of my daughter with these horses?" She asked once.

"Sorry, I cannot paint humans, I don't."

"But why not when you can draw these animals so beautifully?" She asked, bewildered.

"These animals, the mountains, the trees, the river, the sky, everything, but human, Mrs Caspero, EVERYTHING BUT HUMAN is predictable within limits. Everything I will draw about them will be true - true to their nature, true to their roots, true to their natural capabilities and gifts. My paintings can truly

66

relate to them. But a man cannot be trusted to paint his true picture.

A man is the greatest contradiction in himself, of his capabilities; his power; his nature; his wisdom and beliefs.

A man invented the electricity to serve the masses; another man invented the nuclear bomb to blow the masses. A man spread a religion to give people the message of peace and love; another man kills the same people on the name of same religion. A man nurtures his plants to save his next generations and the planet; another man destroys the earth with his greed and narrow vision.

You bring a dog knowing that he will guard your house. You see a snake and immediately you know you have to protect yourself. You see the beautiful birds and know you will admire them. You see the black clouds and pick your umbrella, knowing well it might rain. You dive in water only when you know swimming.

But do you know when the person who wasn't supposed to ever let you down, tears your heart apart? Do you know when you tell somebody a truth, hoping he will empathize with you takes advantage of your situation? Do you know when your honesty gives you nothing but utter contempt and adversity? Do you know when all you want is to live with love and peace, but all you would be offered, is hostility and disgust?

Nothing is definite in your human's world, Mrs Caspero, Nothing. Everything is like a dream in your world. Everything. Every human feeling is like a dream and you never know when you are going to wake up to see that dream shattered. Here every human feeling is like sand; like water; like air; which you can NOT hold in your hand for long, with a sense of relief; with a sense of trust; with a sense of accuracy - it will slip away."

She couldn't agree more for what she had seen. Her eyes were telling a painful journey she had gone through.

9. Paint, Brush And Passion

"The last test match is going to be very interesting", Reeve said leaning on the kitchen top. Joe took out a pack of cashew nuts from a cabinet tucked in the corner of a kitchen, to calm down his stomach butterflies for the time being. He took himself a handful and forwarded the pack to Reeve.

"Aye, this is high time for England to win the test series, after so many years, isn't it?" Joe said, excitedly.

"You would hope so, and it could not be better than starting the winning streak from Ashes itself"

"Yep, winning a series from Australia is always special"

"Absolutely."

"Though a draw will do to snatch the series, but a win will be inspiring", Joe reckoned.

"Yes."

"And if Andy Murray also wins its semi-final on Sat, that will be absolutely mint." Joe managed to mumble, his mouth full of nuts.

"That's right. You really love nuts, don't you?"

"Aye, its marvellous", he said and collected his right hand fingers and touched his lips to make a kissing sound, "Pucchhh!", then he hold a cashew in his index finger and thumb, "beauty!"

"By the way, did you hear anything from Shirley?"

"I have already heard enough from her", Joy replied, tension gripped his face.

"Get over it man. Get over it."

"I wish I can."

"It may be hard but trust me, it is possible. Besides, you have to concentrate now on this new chapter of your life anyway. Medicine is not a profession you can do half-heartedly."

"Don't worry; I am sure, I would not let my personal life effect my professional life".

"Good then, wish you all the best."

"Wish you too."

"When do you have to join the Eastbourne Surgery?" Reeve enquired.

"I am starting from 17th of August."

"Good"

"And you are joining Cornmill primary care trust in July?"

"Yes."

"I wish we could have joined at the same place"

"Oh no, I had enough of you!" Reeve joked and added, "Well, it's only one year training, who knows after that we might be bumping into each other again in the same hospital."

"Yeah, but I think I will stay with you until I sort something out or you kick me out", Joe chuckled.

"Sure, most welcome! After all I need somebody to make me jacket potato and all those lovely stuff." Reeve returned the honour.

"Oh! Pleasure is mine."

Joe opened a can of baked beans and microwave sounded "click". He took the plate out from the microwave and cut the potatoes in half, filled with grated cheese and baked beans and put it back in microwave for half a minute.

Reeve took out the Orange juice bottle from the fridge and asked "Juice?"

"Yes."

Reeve poured the juice into two cups and offered one to Joe.

Joe stood beside Reeve, silently, as if nothing to do, watching Reeve who had then started cleaning of dishes. After a while he said, "By the way, I have seen your new paintings. You've been quite interested in horses lately." He enjoyed seeing his paintings often which Reeve kept in a cupboard in the study room.

"Yes, I am. Any suggestions?"

"No! No! They are fantastic. I was just wondering when somebody else will appear in the paintings, besides the horses. You know what I mean, don't you?"

"That is out of question."

"These horses belong to that horse trainer you met in the hospital, don't they?" He chuckled.

"Yes, they are." Reeve said.

"Umm! I can smell something is cooking between you and that horse trainer." He giggled.

"Yes, something is cooking. But here, right now, in your mind. Nowhere else!"

In last few months, Reeve had painted several pictures of horses, showing different activities and emotions of the animal. He visited the place in Osterley when he wished and left when he liked. Helen or nobody on the farm ever said anything about his visit, as if he owned the place and as if making an appointment to visit there was unexpected.

"You haven't become obsessed with this place or my animals or may be of the smell around it, have you?" Once Helen asked him when she saw him, sitting on a rock in the field and studying the grazing horses.

"Not really. Tell me when you don't want to see me here."

"I didn't say that."

But maybe it was the other way around. For quite some time she was getting obsessed with his paintings. She would come and sit at a distance when she knew that his painting was about to finish and would look at them in admiration. She liked horses but after seeing his paintings, she liked them even more. His paintings had captured some of the finest moments of the animal. Though she had seen and observed all of it already but his paintings had given even more meaning to them. The paintings included a stallion standing tall on his back legs and snorting as if he was reminding of his presence; two horses stabled in the boxes next to each other and talking through a hole in the wall; a foal being fed by her mother; a horse walking proudly through the mud and keeping his head high; and a horse in the air, jumping through the hurdle showing his strength and speed.

That day she was watching him paint from a distance, but it was a different day. The beauty of the painting had aroused her in a way that she never felt before; never dreamt before, and never wanted to have that feeling before. The painting was taking shape and so was her desire - her desire to touch him, feel him and to be a slave of his body; of his power; of his desire. Her body wanted to be dominated by him. She felt weak, tormented and angry– angry, because she had never before allowed her body or her emotions to rule her like that.

She had learnt to channel her emotional energy into physical energy since the age of nine when she would jump on her grand trampoline, for hours until either her emotions were vanished or her body had given up. She was an expert in most of the martial arts and her physical fitness was outstanding. She was wild, intrepid and a strange character to handle. When she was studying, she was labelled as oppositional. Pupils who heard about her never dared to talk her. Pupil who were rescued by her in different traumatising circumstances were never allowed to befriended with her and pupil, who came in her way as a foe, kept silence about her. She never wanted to be a leader among her peers but could not help herself find her in a situation when helping others. She was different from her peers; she hated what girls liked the most. At her age while most girls were crazy about cosmetics, jewelry, boys and shallow gossips she spent most of her time learning martial arts and horse riding. One day when she was sitting on top of the boundary wall of a house, outside of her school, she saw two tall guys were pushing one smaller boy in the corner. She knew he was being bullied and she had an urge to go there. She recognized the boy but the other boys looked outsiders. "What's going on lad?" She asked the smaller boy.

The boy didn't respond out of fear but suspected if she was Helen. He had heard about her but never seen her. His eyes were asking for help. "Hey, chic, what you want?" One of the tall guy shouted at her. She was then in no doubt that something was wrong.

"I want you to leave the boy." She demanded.

Another guy produced a knife from his inside pocket of his jacket, showed it to her, and commanded, "Run away, girl."

She swiftly kicked his knife away from his hand in the air and gave the boys some fine martial art kicks and punches she had perfected over the years. The boys were on the ground in disbelief. The young boy was relieved and asked, "Are you Helen?" After seeing her into action, he was sure of that but still asked, as if asking that was a compliment to her in itself.

Her mother had always encouraged her to do what she wanted to do, since her father had left them. She wanted her daughter to be tough, to be able to fight the difficulties in life lying ahead for her.

Her father had a very successful horse livery business, which he inherited from his father. She loved her father and for her he was the best father in the world. Since childhood she was fascinated about the horses and her father brought her a pony when she was only five. Her toys included either horses or things related to horses. Her mother, Judy, was a fine horse woman too and she had a good eye for the horses. People had often taken her advice when they wanted to buy a race horse or if they simply wanted to bet on a horse in racing. Helen's friends used to come at her farm, to take a ride on a pony or to learn horse riding. When she was nine years old, her friend Sarah and her nineteen years old sister, Sally, started to come to learn horse riding. Helen had requested her father to help learn Sally horse riding. About three months after Sally started learning horse riding, her father suddenly disappeared. After a few days Helen had learnt from Sarah that her sister Sally was also missing. And when Judy found out that a large chunk of the money was also taken out from the banks she feared the unimaginable – her husband had run away with Sarah's sister. "Your father has gone for some work and he will come back after some time", she had told Helen for that she was too young to comprehend the ugliness of its adversity on her life. But Helen had learnt it soon as everybody in her school and village had talked about it. She shivered for minutes when she first learnt the nature of its roots. She felt a gush of emotions that was not fear or a sense of loss or hatred, but distrust - distrust for everybody; for everything; for every emotion. That day, she ran and ran until she fell down and slept. She never let her mother knew that she knew about it. After that she started learning everything which could exhaust her until her last breath, something physical, through which she can vent out her emotions. She learned boxing, Karate, Kung fu, Judo and every other martial art available to learn. She never gave up to the pain and suffering but found a meaningful way in her work and physical exercises to keep her emotions at bay.

When she was seventeen, a man came to her house with a few gift packets in his hands. He was a humble man who told her that he was her father. At that time, she was alone at her house. She ran to the kitchen and returned to the man. She kicked his gift packets away from his hands, grabbed him from behind and put her one hand around his neck. Her second hand pointed a knife towards his chest. "If you ever came again in our life, I'll kill you." She said slowly but with all the seriousness. He never returned after that. It was not fear or guilt but utter disgust —the disgust he felt from himself and his life. Her mother never learned about the incident. But for her, he was already dead. After her father was gone, her mother started a horse training school at which she was good and she produced some of the finest point to point race horses. Helen was also learning the art of horse training. She had a natural talent with horses. She understood their every emotion; every move and every need. And in return they understood her body language and enjoyed her company. They trusted her. She was a born leader amongst them.

Once somebody had asked her, "there are not many women in this profession then why did you choose this as a career?"

"I prefer dealing with an animal than a human". She had replied.

She could easily control the rudest horse in seconds. She rarely needed to use force to train her horses; instead she believed in patience, compassion and natural leadership and used round pen technique instead of severe force to train them. She quickly became famous among horse owners though they didn't like her personally, but they came to her when they heard about her repute with animals. For them she was rude and arrogant but when she spoke to her animals, she was a different person. In her first year as a horse trainer she had produced five national hurdle race winners. She believed in her horses so much that before employing anybody she would introduce them to one of her trusted horse and observe the animal's reaction. If the animal reacted badly she would not employ the person, and only if animal reacted positively she would go further. She had a belief that they possessed a natural ability to detect the inner emotions of an individual. And she was right, most of the time. She had an eye for the race horses like her mother and was very intelligent with pedigrees. Once she spotted a horse, Hard Rock, in a Chelsea National Hunt Sales. Several horses were walking round and round and Hard rock stood out of them. It was an unbroken horse and walking well. She liked its broad shoulders and good front legs. It was a proper athlete from Chris Hart's yard. She investigated about its pedigree and took few pictures of the horse. Later she advised one of her client Gary Evans to purchase that horse. Phil could not deny her judgement and purchased the lot at a huge price. He was rewarded for that when Hard Rock won three National Championships back to back under training from Helen.

Reeve finished the painting, packed his painting stuff and was ready to go when he saw Helen behind her.

They gazed at each other. A raw desire but nothing else existed between them. Not two souls, not two minds, but only two bodies. Desire, only carnal desire, which they had to carry out as everything else; as they ate, as they slept. She stood up and moved towards him. He laid his painting on the ground. They stood face to face, next to each other, as if, taking approval of each other and agreeing on a deal to gratify only and only their bodily desires. She held his hand and started walking. He followed her silently, like an earnest follower. On a fifty yard distance, there was an empty horse box. They entered the box, latched the door from inside and closed the telescopic partition. He pushed her onto the wall and held her hands above her head on the wall from his left hand. His right hand unbuttoned her shirt ruthlessly. She held the bar above her head from both hands. For once she enjoyed being controlled by the man whose intentions were as clear as hers, as loud as she wanted. The clear knowledge and honesty of the intent and such intensity of the joy was incomprehensible for her. She was thrilled, perturbed and then pleased that somebody out there was not intimidated by her virtues or frightened by her will, but was a part of that virtue, that will.

After a while, she sat on a rubber ramp in a corner of the box with her legs folded and hands tied around them. She was enjoying the moments just passed away and yet inside her something, somewhere, she would always have.

10. A Bump

It was more than three months back when Reeve last visited her farmhouse. But he had a dream last night and suddenly he had a desire to see her. He saw in his dream that Helen is hanging on a cliff waiting to be rescued, while giving every ounce of her will power to hold on - just to hold on until somebody comes and rescue her. He was sitting with Joe in a helicopter, bypassing that cliff when he heard a sound, which was neither clear nor likely in those mountain heights, and then he saw Helen. He had lowered his helicopter and anchored her, holding by his hand. He saw her smiling face and her lean angelic body, hanging by his hand. Then he saw the monstrous valley beneath her and the mountains glorifying its depth. He was frightened and uncertain of himself and at that moment, his mind had tricked him and he loosened his grip. He watched her falling down in awe, her hand still pointing towards him, as if, he was still holding her. He closed his eyes and started to loosen his belt. At that moment Joe had called, "Reeeeve! Its eight O'clock now", suddenly he came out of his dream and woke up in a hurry. He had not called her since they last met and neither did she. He was neither under any courteous obligation to see her, nor did he wish so. But then he was ready to go. Helen didn't expect him to come, at least not soon enough. But a part of her wanted to see him and a part of her wanted to forget him and wished that he never came there.

After a long drive, he reached Osterley. He saw her far away patting a horse in the field. He had not brought any painting stuff with him. He didn't want to paint there that day. It was the first time he came there for the sole purpose of meeting her. He walked down towards her. She saw him coming.

"Rookie! You are back."

"I am indeed." He replied.

"You don't seem to be doing any painting today, do you?"

"No, I came here to see you."

"Why you want to see me?"

"I don't know. I am not sure."

She adjusted the saddle of the horse, and sent it away after some petting around its right shoulder. She turns towards him and suddenly, something unexpected caught Reeve's eye. It was a bulge in her tummy. He thought for a moment and said.

"You are expecting a baby?"

"Looks like, isn't it?"

"Hmm!"

In a sudden moment of realization he knew it was he and somehow he felt sure of that. A sense of euphoria was born to him, which was almost new to him. He knew what he had to do.

"So when are you expecting?"

"So do you remember when you last came here?" She snapped back.

He realized his mistake that he has asked a wrong question. He rephrased it.

"Are you happy about this?"

"Let's say, I don't feel sad about anything."

"Don't get me wrong but can I ask you if you are ready for this – I mean, baby?"

"I wasn't, but I am now."

"You won't leave this place, would you?"

"What makes you ask this?"

He paused for a moment and then replied, "Forget it. Do you have a spare room if I move in?" He knew it was out of question that she would leave her horses for him. As a matter of fact – she preferred dealing with an animal than a man, he remembered, she once told him.

"Why do you want to move in?"

"Would you give me some credit for expecting a baby?"

"I guess so."

"Then let me move in."

"I have an empty horse shed, will that do for you?"

"Fine. Anything will do."

"I am joking!"

"I know!"

"Come with me."

He followed her towards the house. Her mother, Judy saw him coming inside and greeted him with excitement, "Oh hello! My dear son, I am very pleased to see you, it's been a while since we last met."

"Yes, indeed. Hope you are not too excited these days."

"Oh, you bet, I am. You see, there is nothing more satisfying then hoping to see your own grandchild."

"Yes, I can understand."

"So where are your paintings today? Are you not going to show me some?"

"No. I came here today to take your permission to intrude in your lives."

"No, you won't intrude in anyway, but what do you mean?"

"Reeve wants to move here with us." Helen explained.

"Oh that is lovely", she moved forward to him and whispered with a chuckle, "May be you will keep her right at last, she doesn't listen me."

Helen gave him a visit of the house. It was a beautiful four bedroom farmhouse with two reception rooms, a study room and a large family kitchen. It had a court yard and a garden with some of the amazing variety of flowers. The four bedrooms were upstairs and they were all good size. One bedroom was converted into a small gym having a tread-mill, a weight bench, a heavy bag for boxing and other fitness equipment. Looking at her gym, it was no wonder; her body looked so beautifully toned and fit.

She took him in the bedroom adjacent to her bedroom.

"Is this room any good for you?"

"It's perfect."

"When are you moving your gears in?"

"Tomorrow?"

"Don't feel any pressure; it's entirely your decision."

"Yes, It is."

He left Osterley after a few minutes and was driving back to his place. It was a long drive and he was enjoying driving down on a straight stretch. He looked calm and composed, as if nothing had happened; as if nothing had changed. Moving to Osterley was the most natural decision for him to take but then it is much easy when one knows what he ought to do.

Reeve was emptying his books from the shelves, into a big box when Joe came in the evening. He looked at the packed boxes in the lounge and then at the Reeve. Reeve continued doing what he was doing, as if Joe wasn't there. It was apparent to Joe that somebody was moving out but the question was that - was he supposed to know what the hell was going on suddenly in that place where he had lived with him for so many years. Joe was about to ask him what was going on when he heard him saying.

"You're just about to get rid of a useless fella." Reeve said with a faint smile.

"And why is that?"

"I am moving to Osterley. "

"Osterley? That horse trainer's place?"

"Yes."

"Hmm! So would you care to tell me why suddenly you decided to move?" He said in a mocking way.

"Not really but if you are dying to know then listen – Helen is pregnant."

"Oh Oh! You mean….Oh man! This is extraordinary.' He laughed excitedly, out of happiness; out of surprise. "You are a man of surprises. I really thought you weren't capable of asking somebody to bed."

"I didn't ask."

"So did she rape you?"

"I didn't say that."

"C'mon! Tell me everything."

"There is nothing except what I told you just."

"So how and when this happened then?" He was persistent.

"Didn't I tell you that everything will happen when time comes?" Reeve replied.

"Yes, indeed, you did." Joe said brightly, He was sad and happy. Sad for himself, for losing his company, and happy for Reeve for at last finding his way. It was a special bond that he had shared with Reeve for last five years, a bond of friendship; of trust and mutual understanding. Since Shirley had left him, he had confided in Reeve for everything. Reeve's utter disbelief in relationships had given him at times some moments to lighten up his own intensity towards his relationship with Shirley, yet he wasn't Reeve to be able to cope with it fully. He was a normal human being with plenty of emotions. And now he had to live alone on his own and he wasn't looking for any new relationship.

It was 8 O'clock when Reeve reached Osterley but it was not as dark as it would be in the month of April. He opened the car boot and started unloading the boxes and suitcases. It was only his books, paintings, clothing and few other belongings, which he took there. Helen saw him coming and asked Paul o help him bring his stuff inside but Reeve insisted that he could manage himself, so he made a few rounds to bring in everything. Judy was pleased to see him. In fact she was even more pleased to see the prospects of her daughter being interested in a man. When she had first known that Helen was pregnant, she was happy that finally Helen was having a relationship but all her hopes had died when she had talked to Helen about it. She had said to Helen with excitement, "Oh my dear Helen! Thank you so much. I am so pleased that I am going to be a grandmother. But I am very angry with you", she had said smilingly, "you haven't told me anything about this man."

"I haven't told you about whom?" Helen had asked her innocently.

"What do you mean by whom?" Judy was really cross then, "I suppose you told me, you are pregnant, so whom do you think I am asking about?"

"Oh I see!" Helen chuckled. "Well, don't worry about him. It was my choice, but I am not having any relationship with him."

"Why so? Is he not a good man? Who is he anyway? Does he have a name? Do I know him?" Judy had shot a string of questions.

"I didn't say that. He must be a nice man, I suppose. But as I said, it was my choice and I wasn't looking for a relationship and neither was he, I guess." Helen defended.

"But what else you need to start a relationship if he was a nice man. Is it not the right time? Besides my grandchild needs a father, doesn't she?"

"It's better not to have a father then having a father like mine."

"Helen! You must not ruin your life because your father has left us."

"I am not ruining my life. I am happy with you and my life. I don't need anybody else."

"But somebody will need somebody, in future."

"Who?"

"Your child, who else."

"I will see then."

"Anyway, are you going to tell me who is he?" She knew all the persuasion would be futile until she doesn't want that for herself. After all, she had grown up a very determined child in Helen.

"You know him."

"But who?" Judy knew Helen was testing her patience.

"It's Reeve."

"Oh lord! That Doctor and a painter! Believe me, I so much wished this to be him and I like him a lot. But I wasn't sure of course. Besides, you have been out quite a lot recently in this racing season, so I was dumb to imagine that you have found someone at last."

"Don't make me pathetic, mom."

"No, I am not. I am just keeping my view." Judy said in a low voice. When Reeve didn't visit for some time after that, Judy thought that it must be Helen who had stopped him from coming over there. But when finally she saw him after a while, she was pleased. And now when Reeve had asked to stay with them and Helen had agreed. She could not welcome the idea less than anyone else.

"Hello Mrs Judy." Reeve greeted her. Judy saw Reeve standing in front of him and suddenly she realized that she was lost in thoughts while sipping a cup of coffee.

"Welcome son! I have prepared your room upstairs, let's go I will show you everything" and suddenly she stopped and added, "Have you had your dinner? I bet you haven't, let me get you something to eat."

"No, I had something when I started. And by the way, I know a bit of cooking, so if you don't mind I would like to bore you both with my recipes from tomorrow onwards."

"No! I am sure your cooking is as good as your painting."

"I won't advise you to keep high expectations."

Suddenly he saw Helen was moving one of his boxes upstairs. He ran with concern to grab the box himself, "Don't you worry about me. It's me who will be worrying for you, if any."

"I am fine, it's not heavy." She tried to convince him.

He had then moved all his stuff upstairs. There was a double bed in the middle of the room and it had an attached toilet that had two entrances, one to his room and the other to Helen's room. One wall in the room was covered with closets and the room had more than enough space to arrange his belongings. Judy had told him that store room downstairs also had lots of space that Reeve could use but he knew he wouldn't need that.

He unpacked his boxes one after another and started arranging the stuff in the closets. After a while, he took the shower. He then put on his night suit and sat relaxed on his bed. The clock ticked as it showed 10 pm but he was neither hungry for a night cap, nor ready to sleep. He looked lost in thoughts. That morning when he had woken up in a busy residential area of London, he had never ever dreamt of moving anywhere and within the next twelve hours he had moved to a farmhouse in the quite suburb of London. But he wasn't thinking about that or the past, it was tomorrow he always mulled about. It was as if time had to catch up with his mind; his planning and his decisions - not the other way around. Next morning he got up early, had shower and prepared the breakfast. He arranged the breakfast on the table before Judy and Helen even got up.

"Boiled eggs and cereal? Who asked you to prepare this breakfast? And I don't take juice in the morning, I will make some coffee." Helen said to Reeve, startled, seeing her breakfast ready.

"I thought you know coffee has a lot of caffeine that won't do much good for you these days." Reeve explained.

"Oh! I forgot, now we have a doctor amongst us." She mocked at him but she knew he was right.

Reeve left after a while for the hospital and returned in the evening with some books. He worked on his laptop for some time and took some prints. Later in the evening when Helen went into the kitchen to prepare tea, she saw a paper was glued on the overhead cupboard near the electric cooker. It read:

Following foods should be avoided during pregnancy:-

#Caffeine – Should avoid during the first trimester but may be taken in moderate quantity later in pregnancy.

#Raw eggs – It may have salmonella.

Deli Meat – It may be contaminated with Listeria, which may cause miscarriage.

The list was long, but she read and understood, and understood that somebody was keeping a close eye on her. She was almost frightened, frightened with the joy she felt. Later when she went upstairs where she had setup her gym, she found another list there, which read:

Few things you must take care, for yourself and the precious life growing inside you:-

#Avoid arching of your back or any exercise involving abdominal strain

#Do not do sit-ups that are past 45 degrees.

#Don't take over exertion! Cut back on your exercise levels as pregnancy develops.

The list was not but as she read and understood, she realized how carefree she had been until now about her pregnancy and how important these things were to her to know, and to take care of. After a brief exercise session, she walked down to Reeve's room. The door of his room was open, yet she gave a light knock on the door. He was working on his laptop set on a table in a corner of his bedroom. He continued working and ignored the knock. "You look pretty busy?" Helen said.

"What do you want?" He looked up at her then. She was wearing a stylish red bra top, which was revealing her marvellously toned muscles of her curvy body, and a black Nike short tight showing her beautiful legs and thighs. Her brown silky hair with a demure collection of curls were tucked beautifully in a voluminous ponytail, placed high on her head were screaming 'confidence'. Bulge in her tummy was giving her a complete feminine look.

"Nothing. I just wanted to tell you that someone is being very concerned about me."

"Or maybe not." He replied.

"Yeah, maybe not, but thank you for these notes you have pasted all over the place."

"You don't need to thank but follow what is right", Reeve said flatly.

She gave him an odd look and said, as if talking to herself, "hmm, it makes us two here."

"And what is this now?"

"I mean, I am not the only one arrogant around here, am I?"

"Is it a compliment? Not that I care."

"I'm not good in giving compliments to anyone. You'd be surprised how much people hate me for this."

"I'm not good at it either – do you hate me for this?"

"Hahaha", she laughed like a child, like a child who was playing hide and seek and her buddy has just found where she was hiding, "No, not at all. In fact, I like you rookie! If I were god, I'll make hundreds of Reeves for me – one as my client who will ask me to train his horses; one as my employee who'll take care of my horses; one on the till when I go to the grocery shop and so on." She said in the way as if she wasn't serious but then she wasn't good in showing friendliness.

"You dream of perfection from your eyes. What you see as right is perfect for you. What you see as perfect is right for you. That is what you wish to see everywhere and in everybody. That is what you want and expect others to see – your perfection, your righteousness. That is what you wish to impose on them. Beyond that, nothing else; nothing more is good or acceptable to you. And that is the ultimate cessation of one's freedom, one's actions you wish for. And that is when you restrict your own freedom to act upon; you restrict the freedom of your own virtues.

You don't need me or hundreds of me; you need only one – yourself. When you'll learn to live without caring for anybody but yourself then you won't need hundreds of me or for that matter me".

She took a moment and then confessed, "I suppose I don't need anyone but I'm sure your company won't bother me either."

"Hmm but at the moment you need a shower more than me, you are sweating like hell."

"I can have both."

"I am at your service."

Then he remembered something, "Oh, I have got some books for you, if you care to read", he got up and took out some books from his leather bag and extended towards her - all of them were on pregnancy.

"I would love to read them but not now", she extended her left hand and held his right hand instead of books. He dropped the books on the bed, moved forward and held her other hand. They came very close and stood in front of each other holding each other's hand, as if two delegations were exchanging a mutually signed agreement. The difference was that they agreed without a paper.

11. An Arrival

On a dry warm day of mid-October when it supposed to be fairly cold days, the air was crisp and the trees were crowded with the brightly coloured leaves. In a countryside of London a rainbow across the dual carriage way was appearing like a welcoming grand entrance for the blue Peugeot which was racing through the dual carriage way. Trees have discontinued the photosynthesis process due to the scarce of sunlight but the bright yellow, orange and red coloured leaves of trees such as oaks, maples and elms were making up for that. Thanks to rather much wet season and the late winter leaves were still hanging around the trees. The beauty of the landscape was capable of delighting even the least worshipper of nature. Reeve wanted to stop the car and breathe the air while drifting through the sun-dappled grassy hills but he continued driving and soon he reached Helen's farm house. Like most of the times, he saw Helen outside observing her horses from a distance. Paul, Carolyn and others were doing various chores which that were needed to be done. She had already completed thirty six weeks of pregnancy and her belly was much bigger then. The big day was just round the corner. In the last few months, she had felt as if she had re-discovered herself – perhaps a softer side of her. She never thought of having a baby but then she was ready for that. She tried to remember when she was so happy but no that was the happiest time she was having. And yet at times, she felt scared; scared of something happening that was out of her control; out of her happiness. In the last few days she had weird dreams and a particular dream that she saw a few days back was still haunting her. She didn't believe in dreams, yet she was trying to make a meaning out of that dream. She dreamt that a fierce battle was going on and she was standing with a baby in her arms in the middle of a battlefield. Warriors were fighting with swords, halberds, spears and the other ancient weapons but nobody was hurting her, as if she was invisible or untouchable and yet she was screaming for help. At that time she had woken up and found herself sweating.

"Enjoying your time?" Reeve came from her behind and asked.

"Yeah, I suppose so. You're early?"

"Yes, I haven't had any emergency today, so I thought let's check on you and see how you're coping."

"That's very kind of you!"

"Why are you sweating?"

"No, I am fine." She said. Two months back, when she had gone for a routine prenatal check-up, doctor had told her something unexpected. Her baby's left kidney was missing and she was going to be born with a single kidney. Later doctor had explained her that this condition is called 'renal agenesis' and about 1 in 650 babies were born with similar condition but there was nothing to worry, as one kidney may be sufficient to function the body and most of the babies often lives normal lives. Although, she would need regular check-ups.

"Is little one not ready to come out yet?" Reeve asked to drift her away from her thoughts.

"I suppose she is as adamant as her father."

"I take this as a compliment."

"Shall we go downstairs, you must be hungry."

"Yes! My belly is telling me my throat is cut."

"I'll prepare something."

"No, I'll prepare," and then he added "I haven't come here for relaxing."

"Then why did you come here?"

"I thought you know that."

"OK, you arrogant fella! So what is on the menu today?

"Something you like the most."

On the way home he had done some shopping as he did most of the time and brought a pie crust shell and some vegetable. Broccoli quiche was Helen's favourite and he had learned to cook it from Judy. When he first came in the house he insisted on preparing the breakfast and evening meal but Judy always woke up early and prepared breakfast and packed lunch for him.

He placed all the ingredients on the work surface and carefully planning the preparation sequence.

Helen sat outside in the hall watching Reeve's every movement, far away in the kitchen. She restrained her urge to go in the kitchen and just talked to him or chip in some way. Though, it reminded her the childhood memories of Judy preparing meal for her as she sat there starving and eagerly waiting for her best food to be served.

After a while, the hot quiche was ready with salad on the large cherry wood dining table with an antique finish. Helen, Judy and Reeve sat on the leather chairs around it. The aroma of her favourite dish had already started enticing her taste buds but then she always seemed to be hungry those days. And that had truly justified the doctors who had said that then she had to feed herself for not one but two lives.

"How do you manage to do everything so quick?" She said while serving food to him and Judy.

"Your horses have given me some of your tips on how to be fast."

"Hmm, you really love cooking, don't you?"

"You think so!"

"I wonder if you have heard people say, men don't eat quiche.

"When you have started caring about what people say?"

"I am talking about you, rookie!"

"I don't listen to rumours."

Judy had been quiet that evening and perhaps she was trying to see her daughter's future beyond to-be-mother. The relationship between Helen and Reeve was not what she had expected. They had maintained a distance between each other and things were not really warming up. She even thought about the idea of leaving them together and moving out herself somewhere but when she discussed it with Helen she had loathed the idea and warned her not to bring any silly suggestions like that in future. She had started planning for her to-be-born-grandchild. For the last few months, she had been busy knitting, stitching and preparing jumpers, frocks, caps, gloves and other stuff for her first grandchild. It was after years that she was involved in some creative work like that and she was thoroughly enjoying it. She had even bought a new stitching machine to prepare the clothes. She didn't know whether it would be a girl or a boy but then anything would suit a baby. Reeve had joked after seeing all the beautiful designer clothes she had made for the baby that she could have opened her own boutique. Helen had suggested her not to worry about anything as they can buy everything from shops but Judy wouldn't listen and had explained her, "it's not about what you can get or not from the shops but it's a way of sharing my love with my grandchild. It's a special kind of joy I would feel when my grandchild would wear them. Do you know, when you were small you had mostly worn clothes made by me?"

"I think that's it, seems like my baby is calling it the day", Helen said, interrupting Judy's thought train and breaking a brief silence among them, on the dinner table.

"Really? You think you're in labour?" Judy said, getting all excited.

"Has it just started? Is it mild? What's the frequency of the pain?" Reeve shot a string of questions.

"No, I am having pain for the last one hour or so but it was quite mild until now."

"Well, you should have told us before, isn't it? It'll take at least an hour to get to the hospital." Reeve explained.

"May be she just wanted it this way…I mean, she doesn't want to bother the maternity ward while a doctor is with us", Judy murmured.

"We need to get moving, shall we?" He almost ignored Judy's little joke.

Within next fifteen minutes, three of them left for the hospital. Judy had already kept a hospital bag ready with all the necessities in it, ready for an emergency departure for the final journey of the baby before he or she come into the world. On the way, Reeve asked Judy to inform the hospital and then he had a joke with Helen, "I know you are a tough cookie but do let me know if you need me to stop the car." By the time, they reached the hospital, Helen was in the advance stage of her labour and yet she managed to keep her composure. After another hour of long labour, a tiny baby girl was finally out to see the world on her own. As nurse declared to Helen that it's a baby girl and wrapped her around in a soft towel, she asked Reeve if he would like to hold the baby first and then have it washed but he pointed towards the basin where new-borns were washed.

He stood straight, relaxed and content with his both hands in his trouser pockets, as if he had just performed a successful operation but the contentment was limited to only two things, the operation and the patient – the relationship with the patient didn't matter to him.

After washing the baby, nurse assumed that he may wish to hold the baby but he merely said, "She deserves her first", and pointed towards Helen. Nurse looked a bit bemused and thought a person who until few minutes before seemed a father-to-be was then looking like a stranger in the room. Helen sat on the bed relieved but eagerly watching her baby in anticipation of holding her, touching her and feeling her. She cradled the tiny, fragile and just over a 7lb weight baby in her arms and looked at her as if the love was reborn to her. She felt liberated and was shaking like a child. She suddenly wanted to cry with joy, pain and hope but couldn't, as if her tears were dried out a long ago and she was no longer able to vent her intense feelings out. Judy was thrilled to see her first grandchild.

"So have you guys decided on names yet for our little treasure?" Judy looked at both of them for an answer; they were all having breakfast. It was almost a week now since she was born but Helen had a little time to ponder on the name. She thought of talking to Reeve about this but didn't, as if it was too personal to discuss this with him.

They sat in silence for a few seconds and then Helen said, "Not really, do you have any in your mind?"

"Well, of course I have to think something if you guys can't come up with any", and Judy added sarcastically, "I can't leave my only grandchild nameless for very long, can I?"

"No, I suppose you can't." Helen nodded in a way as if she was having a laugh.

"How about 'Tracey'? By the way, it's meaning is 'fighter' and without a doubt she will be a fighter like her mother", Judy proposed after a bit of thought, but little did she realise that later in her life she indeed would have to fight for her life.

"Sounds good to me", Reeve said who had been silent until then.

And a 'motion' was passed without any opposition.

"I am moving out of this house tomorrow", Reeve announced to Helen on an evening when they were out in the meadows for a walk with Tracey.

Helen looked at him unexpectedly for an expected declaration. She knew it was coming but 'when' was the question mark. "You came at your will and you can go at your will", she said after a brief pause.

In the last six months Tracey had become a bit stronger and now she was not as fragile as when she was born. Although she was born with a rare kidney condition but till then she was doing well and doctors had ruled out any reason to worry so far. Reeve had been quite mindful about all her needs in all those days. He had regularly checked her in the nights if she was sleeping well and was always the first to get up and see whenever she cried during the nights. After a couple of nights, Helen didn't even bother to get up and see if the baby cried for she knew Reeve would already be there to look after her. He changed her nappies and clothing, bathed her and massaged her regularly. It seemed that her mother's role was confined to only feed her. It was not as if she wasn't interested to do but Reeve was always ahead to fulfil Tracey's needs. And then he was suddenly ready to go, leaving everything on herself.

"You don't need me?" he asked.

"I never needed you". She said briskly. A human being cannot live without loving someone or wanting to love someone but perhaps the absence of that basic characteristic in both of them was the profound similarity and the reason of their understanding of each other.

"I can see Tracey is in safe hands" He teased her a bit.

"At least I am not someone who thinks his duties of a parent are over in a few weeks", She snapped back.

"My duties are not over but I am just not capable of loving anyone".

"Not even to your child?"

"No, not even to my child and I want to go before it's too late for me but I'll always be there when you need me."

"What? You want to go before you start loving your child? "

"Anyway, you would tell me if there is anything with Tracey, won't you?"

"This is not my answer."

"Do you love your father? No, you don't. But you do hate your father because you loved him once too much. I don't hate my daughter and I never would, and it does not matter to me if I love her or not, as long as I can fulfil my duties of being a human. I do remember you telling me that you had abused and ill-treated your father when he last met you; that's because you were hurt and you still loved him. And that was because love sometimes make you demon."

12. The Globe

Surprisingly, the Met Office has been right this time. London was experiencing its biggest snowfall in many years. In last two days, nature had abolished the difference between colours and covered everything with colourless snowflakes. It was a time of joy for children and nightmare for some, especially travellers. The sledges were out of the lofts and the cheerful snowmen with cheeky red noses were aplenty. And if you were out in the open, then you should be prepared to be hit by a snowball or two by teenagers. Joe looked out of the window and then he started reading a local newspaper. It was a Sunday but he was 'on call' that day. He spotted an advertisement in the 'recruitment' section and told to Reeve who was sitting on a couch next to him and was reading a medical journal, "you might want to have a look on this, it seems to me a damn good opportunity".

"What's that?" Reeve murmured while continued reading his journo.

"Globe hospital is recruiting medics to support its top team. You can be sure you'll get the best experience there apart from everything else and also this will save us a lot of driving. I don't know about you but I am going to apply for this", Joe explained with enthusiasm.

"I'll see". Reeve responded. It had been more than six months since he moved out of Helen's place and re-joined Joe and during this time he had called her only a few times. But she never called him herself, as if it was neither required, nor expected.

Within a fortnight of applying for the job, they had received an interview call and then they both were standing in front of a tall building which looked like a modern art gallery. It had a huge garden, full of beautiful and colourful flowers. There were those fine sculptures of a DNA, a brain and a spine. There was a breath-taking heart shaped fountain which was pumping water in and out of its body. A huge pyramid shaped glass structure building stood in centre of all this. A golden globe was shining on pointed top of the building, but it only bore the name 'Globe', 'hospital' word was intentionally omitted.

Reeve and Joe admired the architecture of the building but neither of them imagined at that time that one day Reeve would run that hospital and would have to take some of the toughest and most crucial decisions of his life.

Almost 30 years back, Dr. Neil Beckman started this hospital in at a tender age of 35. And in all those years, the hospital has touched several heights in terms of practice and research. The first ever open heart surgery in the UK was performed by Dr. Beckman in that hospital. Its instrument laboratory had developed a flexible robot called 'Hawk eye' which revolutionised the keyhole surgery. It was capable of reaching the places inside the body with minimum intrusion where visibility by the naked eyes and the reach of the surgeon's hands were not possible. Dr. Beckman pioneered the brain surgery and when he heard the case of two sisters in Peru who were joined by head; he offered to perform the segregation surgery free of cost and went on to perform it successfully. The hospital's modern high tech research facility had done some of the remarkable work on muscle growth. Its patient list included the VIPs and not-so-VIP people from all around the world. The hospital undertook only the most complicated and difficult medical cases in its care. It was no wonder that its reputation for the excellence and the best care attracted only the highly talented doctors from all over the world.

Reeve and Joe stepped in for a rigorous interview process to test their psychological, physical and mental strength apart from their medical abilities and skill levels. Their last grilling was done by none other than Dr. Beckman himself who asked them questions which were only to test if they had the required mental strength and higher attention-to-detail characteristics. Before the interview ended he told them two things; one that they had been selected and second, they would work under him. Joe joined as a physician and Reeve as a surgeon in Dr. Beckman's top team.

Dr. Beckman was an astute businessman and a philanthropist. He never hesitated to let wealthy people put their money in his hospital. He had formulated a more appealing method of charity towards his hospital. He asked his satisfied rich patients to give money in for sophisticated machines and equipment and in return his hospital would take the needy patients free of charge to give them the required care and treatment. Every month the charitable amount available was declared on a notice board of the hospital and a committee would take decision on cases that deserved the most on the basis of their financial adversity and complexity of the case. Dr. Beckman's family included only his wife Jillian and his hospital. During the times when both of them were desperate for a child, their bonding gave them the strength they needed to disperse the natural craving of being a parent. They had long back decided on names for the baby. Yet, after so many years, they had given up on any hope for a baby and both were absorbed in their professional life. Neil had always felt like living with a family in his hospital, and his staff admired and respected him. He had lived his life modestly even though being so rich and having no children, he could have spent lavishly like most of the people in his shoes would do. He never had any desire for luxuries even when he was a child. Though, his family was more than capable to provide whatever their beloved son would have desired. His father had asked once on his birthday, "Tell me son, whatever you wish this year on your birthday". He decided and said, "Dad, can I get a play house that we saw last week in Metro Centre".

He didn't get an answer but a little frown though he knew he would get whatever he had asked for. His sister Louanda has been grieving for that play house since she had seen it at Toy World when last week their family was out on a window shopping in Metro Centre. She already had two play houses of her choice but never played much with them. Her parents knew they should not let Lou have all her way. They always tried to have a balance between keeping their kids happy and being extravagant. But Neil rarely demanded anything for himself. Once her sister saw an advert for a new toy from Sony and had asked Neil, "bruv why don't you ask dad for this?", and he had said, "I will surely, my little Lou", even though he had little interest in that toy. Her sister had used him many times to get things done whenever she doubted if any heed would be paid to her lavish wishes by her parents. Neil always felt proud to see her little sister happy. Though Beckmans always knew behind the scene Lou was playing but how could there be a denial for a selfless wish of a boy who seldom asks for something. If Neil wants to be happy this way, so be it, they thought.

Money had never been an issue for Beckmans. Mr. Beckman had been involved in property development and had around 25 properties in Oxfordshire County and other areas and all had been rented. In the beginning, when he had started sharing his own inherited house he knew he was going to be a property developer. The property prices were relentlessly going high and there was no reason for their fall if not rise in the future. Oxford University was the guarantee of one's investment in properties in that area, as there was a relentless demand for rented properties. Mr. Beckman had invested all his money in his first house and after renting it out he had soon taken mortgage for another property and it went on and on since then. He had an eye for good properties. One could bet on his predictions and he knew how to develop a property in the best possible way. While renting out his properties, he always put his properties on sale at substantially high prices and if a buyer was ready to give that price, Mr. Beckman had nothing to lose and he would develop another one using that money with a huge profit in his pocket. Mrs. Beckman had given up her librarian job when his firm needed a manager to look after his growing business and she soon learned all the secrets of the property business.

Beckmans were well known in elite community of the city. They had a large 4 bedroom Victorian house which included a large soft play area designed with the most advanced play facilities and had a small football court, tennis court, ball room and the slides. Beckmans didn't allow their children to go out much. Beckmans wanted their children to be confined in their house as they wanted to see them playing safe and secure and where they cannot possibly learn the bad things while out to play with other kids. Whenever Neil had asked her mother to go out to play footy, she had replied, "Son you have your own footy court, why don't you invite all your friends here and play with them"

"They will not come; they say their mom won't let them come"

"You don't worry about them; you can play with your father and sister or on your own."

"But mom, I want to play with them. Why they treat me differently?"

"What did they say to you?" she asked, anxiously.

"They say, I am too rich and spoiled"

"But you are not spoiled," she would unsuccessfully try to soothe him.

Neil hated his play area, his toys and luxuries. He wanted to live like other kids, be a part of them and get their company and love.

He never invited his friends to his house and never mentioned his expensive possessions. In school he had been seen as a helping person. He never had any fight, and was always ready to help out his classmates in anyway he could. He will write essays, solve their maths problem and will let them copy in the tests whenever he could. He was an intelligent kid but never showed it off. Jillian was with him in his class since year 8 and both have liked each other. When Jill first time came to St. Pancras School, Neil had shown her every corner of the school. Once Neil invited her to see a Jungle play in which he was taking a part and after the play, he had asked Jill, "Now it's time for you to solve a riddle".

"A puzzle", Jill asked, mystified.

"Yes, tell me, what role I was playing in that 'jungle' play?"

And Jill had replied wisely, "You can't be that tiger who was roaring on everybody; you can't be that beer who was looking so grumpy and you can't be that monkey who was so naughty.........you must be disguised as Giraffe who was so humble and tall." At that time Neil had liked her very much.

When Jill was suffering from Jaundice, Beckmans allowed Neil to visit Jill every day. He went to see Jill after school and as he knocked on the door, Mrs. Ward opened and gave him a warm smile,

"Come-in son, she will be glad to see you".

Her room was decorated in pink and purple and was medium size. Bedside table was full with medicines and drink. Gillian was looking pale but brightened up as soon as she saw him.

"I hope you won't let me get bored in school for long and will join me soon", he said.

"I am ready to be in this bed forever, if you keep visiting me like this," she replied.

"Here I am visiting you and see who is in your eyes always," he said, looking at the picture of the upcoming singer Robbie Young on the wall facing Gillian.

"I wish I can put your picture there" she replied.

"No I don't want to bore you like he does by being in front of your eyes always."

He always brought yellow Orchids for her that she liked most and he would sit with her for hours telling her jokes and all the updates from school. She had other friends regularly visiting her as well but she waited only for Neil.

At the tender age of eighteen, they decided to get married. It was the best decision they had ever taken in their life as since then they had cherished every moment of each other's company.

13. Together We Live Again

Trin' Trin' Trin' Trin'….

Helen leaped at the receiver inevitably. "Talk to me."

"Thank you."

"Thank you for what Rookie?"

"For permitting me to talk to you."

"You never needed my permission to talk to me by virtue of being 'Reeve Harvey'."

"How is Tracey?"

"She is doing well now but she is in the hospital at the moment".

"What happened?"

"She had swelling in her legs, abdomen and face."

"Why didn't you tell me? I asked you to tell me if there was anything wrong with Tracey."

"Yes I know but I didn't promise you anything, did I?

"Alright! So in which hospital is she now?"

"Priestgate Hospital."

"OK, its nine O'clock now and I suppose visiting hours are over for today. I will see you early morning tomorrow?"

"Yeah, see you tomorrow then".

"See you".

It was more than a year ago since they talked to each other. Conversation he had with Helen a day before he had left her place was echoing in his mind.

"At least I am not someone who thinks his duties of a parent are over in a few weeks", she had said, and Reeve had replied abruptly, "My duties are not over but I am just not capable of loving anybody".

Yes, Helen is there to look after her. She is capable and strong but this was not a valid reason to escape from one's own duties, he had thought.

The time he had spent with them was an act out of his own values. It was neither a sacrifice nor an act of kindness. Yet, it was not his values he had escaped from but something which had told him that it was his own creation whenever he had cradled that small life in his arms. Whenever her delicate partly opened eyes had looked at him, she had told him that she needed him. It was something which had told him that she was the purest form of human being before the injustice and inequalities of the world. It was something that told him that loving her would give him the divinity of god. It was all the goodness he wanted to preserve for all his life yet the same craving had weakened him because he wasn't able to comprehend the idea of losing her. It was this weakness he had struggled to leave behind. But now he knew he had to overcome this and yet preserve the goodness.

Kuduk' koooon'…kuduk' koooon'…kuduk' koooon'…The 'irritating' alarm went off at 6am sharp and Reeve hurriedly got up and started to get ready and by 8 o'clock he was with Helen in the hospital.

He entered the room no. 607 on the 6th floor of the hospital and first thing he saw was his daughter's face. Tracey's little figure was lying on the hospital bed. She had yet to complete two years of her life. She was in sleep and her angelic face was personifying 'innocence'. He looked at her intently as if she was talking to him – asking him that where he had been and why he had left her alone. It was the most beautiful face he had ever seen. It was a feeling he rarely confronted with; rarely known to him but it was much of a pain than guilt.

"Do you have doctor's report? What did he say?" He asked Helen who was sitting next to Tracey's bed and looked withdrawn.

"No it's not with me. It has something to do with kidney, I don't remember the medical term they said, but doc says she will be OK after medication", Helen mumbled.

"And how Tracey has been coping?"

"She is coping well, but I think she felt a bit insecure here so she cried even if I left her for a second", and then she added, "do you think Tracey's problem is related to her single kidney? Is single kidney not sufficient for a body to function? And what these bloody kidneys do anyway?" Helen asked irritably.

"I can't say, until I've seen the reports, It looks like a 'nephrotic syndrome' in which kidney fails to retain protein and other substance from the blood and leaks it into the urine. Regarding your second question - a kidney is like a filtering system of the body which disposes of the waste products like extra water and return the required chemicals back into the body. Beside this, a kidney also produces some vital hormones like rennin, erythropoietin and active form of vitamin D which helps in regulating the blood pressure and the levels of minerals and calcium. Normally, a person can do with only one kidney but sometimes problems do occur with single kidney". He explained to Helen.

"Right! Tell me honestly, this is not a serious problem, is it?"

"No, I don't think it's a serious problem. By the way, I've joined Globe hospital few months back. If she doesn't recover soon, we can move her there, if you don't mind. They have a really good Nephrology section there, besides I can keep an eye on her in the hospital. I think she will now need regular check-ups anyway."

"No, I don't mind if this is the best thing to do for her."

"Good. And I have something more to say."

"Go on then."

"What if I suggest you that we take a house that is near my hospital and then you can move in with me there?"

"Why is the change of heart? You moved out once, didn't you?"

His answer had a touch of intense graveness, yet he bore a hint of smile, "Yes, indeed. That was good for me. This is good for all of us. Or you can say that I was selfish in doing that but then I am selfish even today. Only thing is that this selfishness is greater than the one I had."

She looked at him closely. He didn't look like a man who was suffering but a man for whom suffering was worth.

"What if I deny the offer?"

"You are as free as I was and you know that."

"I know. I have to think about this and talk to mom."

"I could live with you at your place but as a doctor it's not advisable for me to live very far from the hospital. I have to be 'on call' frequently."

"Yes, I understand."

14. Tracey

10th December' 1993

Judy put a violin shaped cake on the table, next to Tracey's bed and lit the candle which was in the shape of number 'six', as she had turned six that day. Helen, Reeve, Joe, Dr. Ravi Patil, Dr. Neil Beckman, a few nurses and others who were very close to Tracey gathered in a good size private room of the Globe hospital to celebrate Tracey's birthday. Tracey was wearing a yellow and red frilled dress which Judy had made for her. Even after Tracey's birth, Judy had continued preparing dresses and jumpers for her. She was a real master in the art of knitting and tailoring. She prepared herself almost all of the dresses Tracey wore since she was born. At the age of 55, Judy was a computer savvy and sometimes she searched different design ideas for the dresses and woollens on the internet and then replicated those designs with her own hands. She was also fond of creating pictures and beautiful greeting cards and send them to people. She loved photography and made good use of her digital camera which Helen had gifted on her 51st birthday so that she could take as much photographs as she wanted. In the last four years, she had taken hundreds of photographs of Tracey and everyone. She had got framed some of the amazing pictures and put on their front room wall.

It was Tracey's 3rd consecutive birthday she was celebrating in the hospital. In the last three years she has been in and out of the hospital on a regular basis.

She had been suffering with multiple symptoms of Nephrotic syndrome which was causing her body to lose large amount of protein through the urine. Dr. Patil who was one of the leading Nephrologists in the country was taking care of Tracey's case. He had explained that this syndrome was a result of an autoimmune disorder and that the immune system in a body protects against microorganisms and other 'foreign' substances. He had explained further that when a person suffers from the autoimmune disorder, his body's immune system attacks its own tissues as it cease to recognize one or more of the body's elements as 'self' and creates antibodies that attack its own cells, tissues or organs which results in harm and inflammation in the body.

But perhaps all the knowledge he had given to Helen about the disease seemed mere a waste to Helen when he had told that the exact cause of autoimmune disorder were still unknown. For a doctor, using words such as "no cure" or "unknown disease" was the hardest thing to do yet he'd hoped that Helen's diminishing hopes would be kept alive on knowing that he was part of the research team at Globe hospital on autoimmune disorders. Perhaps, it was a wishful thinking on his part about a mother who had been frequently in and out of the hospital since her daughter's birth and whose daughter needed to be continually monitored for life long.

"Now, blow the candle my dear". Judy instructed Tracey who was looking all so excited and ready to swing into action. Her illness had rarely let her spirits down as she always wore her ever so charming smile and kept herself busy in her innocent activities. During her time in hospital, she had nothing much to do and she had found a way to defeat her boredom. She was amazingly talented in solving jig-saw puzzles and at less than four years of age she had solved more than 200 pieces puzzles on her own. It was amazing to see how fast she was; her hands will magically pick only the right piece and put into its place.

She blew the candle and lightly ran the knife on the cake but her fragile hands couldn't cut the cake. The years of diet restrictions and medicines had resulted in a massive weight loss of her that had weakened her. Helen quickly supported her hand to cut the first piece of the cake. Everybody chorused the 'Happy Birthday' song and clapped. Yet, another birthday was done in a

THE SAVIOUR – NEVER LETS HER GO

confinement of four walls of hospital room. Helen and Judy put small pieces of cake in Tracey's little mouth and she then happily returned the favour. Reeve stood in the last row of the small crowd and watched everybody in a sombre mood. Suddenly, Joe realized that and pulled him in and asked him to offer cake to Tracey. Judy served the cold drinks, pies, cakes and cookies to everyone in paper plates. She had arranged everything meticulously for Tracey's birthday.

Tracey started opening her gifts. She looked ecstatic and contended but then it wasn't very often that she had an opportunity to enjoy her life to the fullest. Most of the times she was only a patient, trapped in her bed. She didn't have any friend in school as she had to miss her school quite often due to doctor's appointment or for other reasons related to her illness. But in the hospital, she had charmed everyone with her smile and sweet talks. Dr. Joe who was her physician and uncle and Dr. Patil who was her Nephrologist, soon became her best friends. Amusingly, she had given a new name to Dr. Patil - Dr. Pill - she had started calling him. The reason was simple. For every problem Tracey would have, she knew Dr. Patil would add at least one new pill to her medication. But he liked it, for one, he loved the kid and second, at least his name was not misspelled or mispronounced as usually was the case.

She opened a box, wrapped beautifully in a shining wrapping paper, and found her favourite thing and exclaimed, "Sponge bob puzzle, thank you Uncle Joe". That is how she called Joe, 'Uncle Joe'. If "Dr. Pill" was her best mate to have fun, "Uncle Joe" was her mentor in every respect. Joe made a point to spend some time with her every day whenever she was in the hospital. He taught her to cope with her pain and desperation and she spent most of the evenings telling him, what she had done in the whole day. A typical conversation would start with Tracey telling her own mistake, "Today, I was running around the hospital and Nurse Julie was saying 'Go, go in your room, go in your room', but I didn't go." Joe would say, "So, you've been naughty today?" And Tracey would accept innocently, "yeaaaaaaahh, I was being nauuughtttyy. Nurse was saying gooo, gooo, but I didn' goo. Now I won't do this anymore, it's naughty thing to do hun?" Joe liked this absolute innocence about children and she was special for him. She was like her own daughter but then Reeve was like his big brother for him. At times, he inevitably thought of Shirley and wondered had they been together, perhaps he too would have had children. One or two maybe around the same age as Tracey. He preferred to be in night duty when she was in the hospital, so that he could look after her. Tracey's mom and dad were at home but she had another parent in Uncle Joe in the hospital. He read her story books about 'Cinderella', 'Snow White', 'The Sparrow and his four children' and many more and she expressed varied emotions as they both go through the story. Her emotional quotient seemed to be higher for her age. Her questions were innocent yet intelligent and unique. Perhaps she had grown out of her age after spending most of her time in the hospital with people much older than her age. And perhaps that explained that why she enjoyed competing with Uncle Joe in building puzzle blocks and other games and amused herself having a chuckle with Dr. Pill.

15. A Hope

It had started raining a bit faster than it was in the morning. The medium pace of the rain dropping on the concrete pavement and the grass of her back garden were sounding like the noise of some cuisine simmering hot in a giant pan. The wildflower meadows Helen and Judy had created painstakingly alongside the garden walls were shining gracefully while soaking in the rainwater.

Sitting on a folding chair in her garden shed, Helen wondered how many more birthdays poor Tracey has to celebrate in the hospital room. Those five years had been dreadful for her. It was not just the physical side of it she had to cope up with, but the emotional side of it which was not easy to bear. It was a time when she would have enjoyed watching Tracey grow up happily but instead she had been busy hiding her anxiety from her only child. When she should have been taking her to the nursery; to the play centers or to the library - she was taking her to the doctor's clinic or hospitals. When she should have been giving her a variety of foods to try, she was tied up with her restricted renal diet. When she should have been telling her a bedtime story, she was busy calling hospitals to check whether she had taken her medicine or meal on time. When she should have been busy watching her favourite cartoon 'Sponge Bob' with her, she was taking her 'urine' sample, checking her blood pressure and temperature. There were not any easy answer to those things, yet she wondered whether there would be a 'normal' life for them in the future. At that point it looked as possible as pigs flying; unless something changes tomorrow.

"Mom! Are we going somewhere out on this Christmas?" Tracey asked, coming from behind. She had just been relieved from the hospital after being admitted a few days before her birthday.

Helen's thought train abruptly came to a halt and she replied, "Umm! Darling, we've lots of surprise gifts for you this Christmas and my darling is going to enjoy a lot this Christmas."

"Do these surprise gifts include holidays?"

"No, no! Anyway tell me what you would like to have in dinner tonight?"

"Mom, I know, we aren't going anywhere, that's why you're not answering me."

"Oh! I'm so sorry love, we can't go! Do you remember what Dr. Patil said?"

"No, but why can't we go out?

"Darling, he said that you're on immunosuppressant these days and that means you're highly susceptible to infections, so I'm sorry darling, it's not a good idea to go out! But don't worry; as soon as you're fit enough, I promise, we'll plan some holidays."

"But I'm fit enough now."

"I know you're, darling. Do you know how much mom loves you?"

"That much", Tracey spread her hands wide.

"And that's why you have to trust mummy and I know you would, won't you?"

Tracey given her an assuring nod but it was difficult to tell who was swayed.

Either.

Both.

Nobody.

It was only two days before the Christmas. Tracey wanted to arrange a sleepover party on Christmas Eve and she had already chalked out the plan for the night with her friends, and the girls were confident that they would get the permissions from their parents to stay. Although, Tracey was too young for this but Helen had not objected. One, it was not often that Tracey has a chance to do what she wanted to do, and second, Tracey seemed to had grown out of her age anyway. *She can manage little wild kids*, she had amusingly thought. She had discussed this with Reeve, "I'm allowing Tracey to have a sleepover party on Christmas Eve."

"That's good", he replied.

"You've no more to say?"

"I'll never doubt your judgement and you know that."

"One of your many virtues, Rookie!"

"So you say."

But perhaps Tracey was not lucky enough to get that arranged. First, Melina's, then Ella's and then Abby's mom had called to inform that their daughters won't be able to come for one or another feeble reasons. The actual reasons were anybody's guess. Were they scared that their daughters were too young for a sleepover party? Or were they scared that they might catch some bug with the girl who was so often ill and hospital was known as her second home? Whatever was the reason, they couldn't be blamed for wanting their kids wellbeing, could they? *Every parent has a right to take the best decisions for their kid's interests*, Helen grimly thought. What if, she is not having a sleepover because the bloody bug might catch her friends? What if she can't go out for an outing because the bloody bug might catch her? Damn it! Damn it! She shouted in her heart yet she could feel the intensity of her anger as her body trembled.

But in the end all it mattered that they enjoyed the Christmas Eve. They sang carols, played piano and board games together as a family.

Helen was about to serve the Christmas lunch and Judy was helping her out. Reeve and Tracey were already sitting on the dinner table, waiting in anticipation. Tracey was playing the music by drumming the knife and fork on her china clay plate. Then there was a knock on the door. Helen gestured them to stay put as she was taking the call. She opened the door and there was a man in Santa Claus's gown, he smiled and sneaked around realizing there was a child inside. He took his bag off his back and opened it. But as soon as he saw the content of it, he gasped in horror, frowned and shouted, "Where are my toys?" Helen too shouted in disgust as she saw the heap of medicines, instead of toys.

She checked the clock. It was only 5am in the morning, and again she was up so early. In last few weeks, a series of such bad dreams had started haunting her. She quickly realized that it was Christmas that day. She didn't want to sleep again though she had slept late last night. The night which was supposed to be Tracey's sleepover night instead, she was watching the 'Sponge Bob' recordings with her till late that she had recorded for her during her stay in the hospital, like she always did so she don't miss out. She moved the curtains aside to look out of the window. The snow fall had just begun, she tried to remember when was the last time they didn't have a snowfall on Christmas but couldn't. It was like a ritual, having a snow fall on every Christmas. She enjoyed watching snowfall. It was as if god was trying to soothe the hardness of her mind and body with the soft white wool. She wanted it to be wrapped around her and be invisible for few moments, away from the invisible cruelty of the world, or the visible worldly things.

She realized Tracey was also mad about snowfall but she had slept late last night and Helen didn't want to wake her up so early. Perhaps, there'll be enough snow for Tracey to enjoy making snowman, she expected. And her conviction seemed to be right; snowfall was getting heavier by that time. It was still only 6am, she had rechecked the gifts she had hidden under the Christmas tree. Judy had bought a big Christmas tree for them and decorated it. She was staying with them for the Christmas. Helen was missing her horses, the beautiful countryside view and the fresh open air of her farmhouse but she had already planned to go there with Judy and Tracey in the evening. At least, it'll be a bit of outing for Tracey as well, she thought. It was now 7am and she decided to wake Tracey up then, as snowfall continued.

Helen and Judy were busy preparing the Christmas lunch. They both were preparing several cuisine separately but one common thing they had heavily in their minds was Tracey's diet restrictions. Judy was preparing light and crumbly Christmas cake and roasted potatoes. She had peeled and soaked the potatoes in water overnight so that most of the potassium could be dissolved in water. Helen was preparing the roasted turkey and apple pie. The menu was limited as the last thing they wanted to do was to tempt Tracey to eat things she couldn't have or let her have more than her body can accept gracefully, which was a shame as a Christmas dinner was supposed to be lavish and unrestricted. Moreover, the diet restrictions were confusing and vague. Helen had tried to understand it from Tracey's dietician but after a long discussion, she thought either she was dumb herself or the dietician was super intelligent or probably for few things in life there were never any easy solutions.

"So basically, what food she needs to avoid?" she had asked to clarify the things once more.

"She needs to avoid the foods which are high in phosphorus, sodium and potassium and she also needs to limit her protein and fluid intake."

"Let's start from phosphorous – what are the foods she should avoid for this?"

"All the dairy products ie; milk, cheese, yogurt etc. and also eggs, nuts, beans, peas, bran cereals are high in phosphorous."

"So do you mean she should avoid all these things?"

"I'm not saying this but she should try to avoid or limit these things."

"But you also said that her body needs more calcium and most of the dairy products and the other things you've said are good source of calcium, aren't they?"

"I know. You're right. Unfortunately, most of the foods which are high in phosphorous, are high in calcium as well so she has to take a balanced diet because high level of phosphorous leads to loss of calcium which may cause bone damage."

"What about protein? As far as I know, her kidneys are leaking a lot of protein so why she needs to limit the protein intake when her body needs more protein?"

"I know this is complicated. You're right; protein is the most essential requirement for our body's growth and maintenance. Having said that, since kidneys manage the waste products from protein, large amount of protein will generate more waste which body cannot flush out if kidneys are not functioning well, which in turn will be harmful for the body."

"Okk", Helen didn't sound much convinced though, and what about sodium and potassium, which foods she should avoid?

"Our body needs some Sodium and it is found in almost in all the food, but when kidneys are not functioning well, extra sodium is not removed from the body which causes thirst, that makes you drink more, and drinking lot of fluids in kidney disease may be unsafe as it may cause high blood pressure and swelling of body parts. But by avoiding table salt and salted food we can control the amount of sodium. Similarly potassium is also found in most of the foods and is required by body but when kidneys are not working, high potassium level may cause heart problems. Main foods to avoid for controlling potassium intake are potatoes, tomatoes, milk, yogurt, raisins, peanuts and various fruits and vegetables."

"Doctor, why don't you give me a list of food items which she can have or which she can't have, please?

"As I said earlier, she can have everything in a small quantity as part of a balanced diet. I can give you the average daily amount of everything she needs but it may have to change as per her condition."

"That'll be fine, thanks." She realized there was no point of discussing it further but she had to dig it up herself to know more about the renal diet. In last five years, she had learned that it paid to be little more educated beforehand about the subjects that doctors were going to talk about.

"Mommy, nana was telling that we're going to farmhouse in the evening?" Tracey asked Helen.

"Yes, that is right."

"But you've said that I can't go out."

"Yeah but I've had a chat with Dr. Patil and he said that it should be OK, besides we won't be out for long."

"Fabulous! What more can I ask for Christmas than seeing my lovely horses?" Tracey exclaimed.

"Oh! You're so like your mother! Do you know when your mother was a child, she never ate food without making sure that horses have had their food and she was as mad about horses as you?" Judy shouted from kitchen, overhearing their conversation.

After talking to Tracey, Helen walked towards the study room where Reeve was reading a medical journal. Legs of the wall clock were inching towards 11am but he had not come out of the room since he entered at around 9.30am after doing his daily morning rituals and breakfast.

"Rookie, do you still belong to this world?" she teased him knowing well, he won't be provoked?

"Unfortunately, I certainly do. But tell me - am I still a rookie?"

"Yes, for me you'll always be a 'rookie'." she paused for a second and added, "OK, I will call you Neo, if you feel ashamed of calling you a 'rookie'."

"No, I am shameless! But why would you call me Neo?"

"It's a short form of Neophyte. It has the same meaning as 'rookie' but nobody will know this, so don't worry; it will be our little secret." She chuckled.

"That's hell of a secret." Reeve replied, indifferent to her creativity.

"OK, before I forget, are you coming with us in the evening to the farmhouse?"

"I don't think so, unless you want me to come?"

"Don't YOU want to spend some time with your daughter? Don't you love her?"

"How many times you're going to ask me this?"

"Until, you've lost your patience and replied me truthfully."

"What matters to you? To love somebody or hate somebody?"

"I certainly don't want you to hate her."

"Exactly! Have you ever seen a person hating a stranger? Have you ever seen a person hating whom he has no relationship? A classmate hates other classmate; a roommate hates other roommate; a man hates his own neighbour; an employee hates his own colleague; a brother hates his own brother; a man's heart is broken by his own girlfriend whom he loved most; a parent's heart is broken by their own children whom they gave birth. Hate enters our heart in disguise of 'mates', 'relationships' and 'love'. The very association of these words bring with themselves expectations, bitterness, jealousy, resentment and distrust among humans. Have you ever seen two children sitting on either end of a see-saw going up and down? That is love and hate which changes its position from one to another. The stronger and higher love goes, the weaker and lower love has to come. If only a human can break that association and sit on the centre of equilibrium where he sees unbiased and impersonal view of everybody and everything, it is when, his horizons are open and wide, without prejudice and without love and hate; where he speaks his mind and nothing else; where he does everything to the best of his capability and knowledge; where he has no friends and foe; where he is on his own and that void is a completeness in itself. That is the ultimate state of nirvana. That is my Nirvana."

That evening, Helen, Judy, Tracey and Joe went to farmhouse. Helen had told Tracey that her dad had some urgent case to study so he won't be coming. Joe had come over for Christmas dinner as part of their family.

16. Father And Son

Reeve opened the chest cavity by making an incision through the breastbone, known as 'sternum' in medical term. He then separated the ribs and carefully removed the heart by replacing it with a 'heart-lung machine' without suspending the blood circulation in the body. A device was inserted into the jugular vein in the neck to measure the heart functions and a breathing tube was also inserted into the mouth and down the windpipe to maintain the airway. The heart-lung machine, which was protecting the life of the patient, was a complicated, movable piece of kit which had a reservoir to take the blood from inferior vena cava, an oxygenator to infuse blood with the oxygen and a pump to send the purified blood, back to the heart through superior vena cava. It was illustrating the brilliance of the human mind that the heart was replaced by mere mechanical components developed by human itself. On the other hand, it was evident of the divine power who has installed so many and so powerful and yet compact pieces of kits in a human body which people often fails to realize and utilize in a positive way. Reeve often wondered how much space and how many equipment would be needed to replace just the main parts of a human body and could it ever be replaced by artificial means in a real sense?. If a heart, about a size of a fist, which generally lasts for lifetime without any electricity or batteries, was replaced by a machine which was at least 1000 times bigger than it and which can be used only as a temporary measure; then, how many camcorders will be required to replace two eyes which combined, were the size of an egg and which take live pictures almost throughout one's life time; or how many supercomputers will be required to replace a human mind, which is almost a size of a half football, to store and process the information a mind takes in, in one's life time; or how many dialysis units will be required in once life time to replace the two kidneys, each about a size of a fist, which filters almost 200 litres of blood per day, Reeve wondered.

The man, who was under Reeve's knife, was 56 years old and had been called in emergency for a heart transplant and was suffering from cardiomyopathy. His 26 years old son had asked Reeve just before the operation, "Doctor, is there any complications in this operation? My father will be alright, huh?"

"Transplant is the best hope for your father, and he's got that now, so it's all good at the moment. Rest we've to wait and see." Reeve had replied.

"How long do you think he's to stay in the hospital after this? He had probed further.

"I would say one to two weeks, but we can keep him longer, if you don't need him." He said with a hint of smile.

"Uh-huh! Thanks Doc."

"So you want us to keep him longer?"

"No, no, I don't mean that."

"Never mind".

That transplant was about to give his father a new hope in life, yet, just a few hours ago a family had given up their last hope and agreed to remove the life support from one of their loved ones who was in comma for the last forty five days, and donated his heart and other organs to save other's lives. Sadly, It was one's gain and other's loss!

There were only five men in the operation room and one of them was Dr. Neil Beckman who was overseeing the surgery. Reeve was performing his first open heart transplant surgery independently, since he joined Globe hospital five years back. In last five years, he had performed several kinds of surgeries including heart surgeries but it was his first surgery in Globe hospital's dedicated transplant centre. Reeve had become Dr. Beckman's most trusted lieutenant in the hospital. It was not his consideration but disapproval of the things which others dared to disagree with him; it was not his politeness but frank analysis of a situation; it was not his traditionalist views but the 'out-of-box' solutions; it was not his undue deliberations but the briskness in his actions that inspired Dr. Beckman to consider him worthy of learning his every medical ability and 'trick of the treads' he knew from more than 35 years of his medical career. Reeve had been continually promoted in the rank and this year he was successfully persuaded by Dr. Beckman to become a member of the hospital board of directors. Reeve was the youngest member on the board of directors. He was a quick learner and within a short span, he had mastered the art of most types of surgeries. Many senior doctors were astonished seeing his confidence and smooth movements of hands, while operating on a patient. He was lucky to perform his first heart operation sooner than expected, and that day Dr. Byrne was so impressed with him that he cheekily started calling him 'Showman'.

The stage was set that day, for a fifty years old patient to go for a heart surgery for implantation of a pacemaker. It was a small electronic device which was usually inserted under the collarbone, to regulate the heartbeat by sending electrical signals to the heart. Dr. Byrne was on his desk reading the patient's file before going to the operation theatre. He extended his right hand for the glass of water on his desk, while his eyes stayed put on the file but he misjudged and dropped the glass of water on his desk, breaking the delicate glass, and water quickly spreaded all over his papers on the desk. He panicked and wounded himself from the glass while he tried to remove it from his bare hands. It was a very awkward moment for him since his patient was ready to be operated within minutes and he was then unable to operate due to his injury. Reeve stepped in and offered to do the operation under his guidance and Dr. Byrne agreed on his offer, after discussing the matter with Dr. Beckman. Reeve had seen this surgery performed only once when last time he assisted Dr. Byrne while he operated onto the patient, yet he operated, as skilfully as Dr. Byrne would had.

Dr. Beckman was so confident about Reeve's skills that he handed him a project to develop a mechanical heart in collaboration with a company called 'Life Aids', a pioneering company in medical devices. The artificial heart was mainly to replace the need of heart transplants as there was acute shortage of heart donors. That device had to be more than a 'pacemaker' which was available in the market at that time. That was the time when Reeve got involved in the heart transplant unit of the hospital.

And yet there was a price for him to pay for all this, as if nobody could be immune to flipside of one's goodness, life had to offer. Reeve had successfully managed to make few enemies during his journey of successes and appreciations. Some of his colleagues considered him as arrogant, inconsiderate and insensitive. It didn't matter much to them that he went to great lengths to cure some of his patients. Once a building worker who had fallen while working on a construction site, was admitted after sustaining the major back injuries and wanted to commit suicide, as he had no means of living without his health. Reeve went to America on his own expenditure to get a special steel frame for him so that he was able to stand and walk with the help of a stick. A patient, who was earlier looking forward to a suicide was then making plans for his new life, with a renewed sense of hope and courage.

Reeve was getting ready to perform his second surgery of the day. Nurse Heidi was in his chamber to take the instructions while he scribbled some notes on the patient file. It was a lung cancer surgery and the patient was in his mid-thirties. "Have you checked personally that all the equipment, instruments and medicines required for this operation are accurate and ready?" He asked the nurse. That was his usual question before performing an operation, he asked without any exception to the concerned nurse. Although there were many safe guards to make sure that everything was in order before an operation but having minor glitches during an operation was not a highly unlikely situation and he never preferred that.

"Yes, I had. Everything is OK." Heidi replied.

"Is blood been delivered from the blood bank?"

"No, but I've just called them and it'll be delivered in next few minutes."

"I would like you to go their personally now and see it's done."

"But we still have half an hour in operation."

"Yeah, but we won't have half an hour, after few minutes," he commented - so softly, as if he was talking to himself.

"Yeah, I'm going now." Heidi replied and gave him an oh-that-guy-is-so-difficult look but the blood bank was only two floors down and she didn't mind a walk down there.

After Heidi has was gone he started concentrating on the file, he was seeing earlier, but then his telephone started ringing. He picked the receiver after a few rings and said, "Hello, Reeve here."

"Reeve, its Jim. Have I surprised you? I got this number from Helen." His brother said.

"You have indeed. Tell me?"

"I and Jessica want to see you and it's an urgent matter."

"OK. I'll call you later when I'm free."

"Have you ever been free for us?"

"I can't answer that but you're welcome to take the best message out of it and act upon it. I shall call you later." Reeve put the receiver down without waiting for the answer.

It had been more than 7 months since Reeve had last spoken to him in a party thrown by Jim to celebrate his new house. Perhaps the parties were the only occasion Reeve met his family. He always tried to attend the parties whenever he was invited, despite the occasional public contempt he enjoyed by Jim or his sister, Jessica. Once in a dinner party, after taking a few glasses of wine, Jessica had even surprised Jim, but only in a pleasant way. She had said, "They say, you're lucky if you can escape rounds of doctors and lawyers. Look at my bro! We've got a bloody doctor in our house," and she had thrown her dessert cup on Reeve's face who was sitting on the next table. "Looks like, I'd eaten enough for tonight, so I shall leave you all to enjoy," Reeve had said and quietly left the party. He felt no contempt for them, as if they were only worth ignoring, not worth a reaction. When Jim organized the next party, he didn't want to lose out to her sister in attempt to contempt Reeve. He'd grabbed the mike and announced, "Listen, listen, listen! Here is a mobile number please make a note of it. It's my brother's number, who is of course a doctor and call him whenever you need to see a doctor and he'll only be too glad to be at your service, in middle of the night or on a rainy day – twenty four seven. And please give him a round of applause for his kindness." Jim often had thrown parties, flaunting his money. Jim was a marketing manager in a medical devices company. He was offered that job, after he made claims that he could get big orders from Globe hospital through Reeve. But soon company and he had realized that they were living in a fool's paradise; yet his company had restrained itself in throwing him out, considering the reputation of the Globe hospital, and his rising star Dr. Reeve and thinking that, may be, just maybe, someday this relationship might help the company in big way.

One day, Jim had called Reeve and said, "Reeve, can you see me tonight? There is a good proposition for you."

"What time?" He kept it brief, as if he had sensed everything without being said.

Later that evening when Reeve went to see Jim, Will was on Jim's side.

"Reeve, guess what? I've joined SurgiMagic and I think you know well that they manufacture all sorts of consumable and non-consumable medical products. And here is my proposition – my company will bid for these items in your hospital and you'll help me passing this tender. You'll get five percent neat commission, company and I will be benefited of course and everybody is a winner. And don't worry; they have got the best products."

"It's not a problem then, they will pass the bid."

"Good, then you'll help us?"

"I didn't say that."

"What do you mean?"

"You said, they have got the best products then I'm sure Globe hospital will have no problem in passing their tender anyway."

"Practically, things don't work that way. You ought to help me. You approve things there, I know that." Jim said in desperation. Suddenly he seemed to be polite and respectful to his brother.

"I think you should help Jim, if you can in anyway." Their father, Will, joined the conversation defending Jim.

"Right! I shall leave now. Let me know if you need money Jim, I'll send you a cheque." Reeve got up and started to move out.

"What do you think? You're a big doctor in a big hospital so you won't help me. Let me tell you, you're useless and nobody likes you and one day your hospital will throw you out." Jim shouted at Reeve. He wanted him to react. He wanted to be reproached by him. He wanted Reeve to join in his anger, his desperation and become a part of him. Just like him. He almost begged him to join in by continuously shouting at him but he was too busy to realize that Reeve had already left.

After the operation, Reeve made a call to Jim, "Tell me, what the urgency is?"

"I thought you're too busy to remember us."

"What is that?" He demanded.

"Meet me tonight 6pm at my place."

"I'll be there." He replied and hung up as if uttering a single more word than required would be disrespect to it.

He reached at Jim's place sharp at 6pm. Jessica has not come yet.

"Jessica is running a bit late. Take a seat – relax!" Jim announced.

"How much?"

"15-20 minutes may be."

"I understand that you won't talk without her."

"You got it."

Jessica arrived after half an hour. She worked as an administrator in a software company and that day she had to stay back till late as her boss had an urgent meeting.

"Dad was having a stomach pain for few days and had a scan yesterday." Jessica started talking.

"Hun-Hun?"

"He's been diagnosed with pancreatic cancer." She said slowly.

"What else? Did they tell what type of pancreatic cancer it is?" Reeve probed.

"It's Exocrine. Doctor has said that it's incurable and he should expect to live no more than six months or so".

"Have they done any biopsy?"

"Not yet. The biopsy was scheduled for today but dad didn't want to go."

"What did he say?"

"He says, I've only six months and I don't want to waste my time making rounds to the hospital. He wanted to see you. Besides, we thought maybe you can help us."

"Where is he now?"

"He went to see his friend; we didn't tell him that you were coming."

"Hmm. I'll come again tomorrow to meet him."

Next day when Reeve went to see his father, he had a box of medical instruments with him.

"Good to see you Reeve." Will greeted him.

"Good to see, dad."

"How is Tracey, Helen?"

"Not bad."

"Tell them to meet me sometime."

"I will."

"I want to tell you that I'm very proud of you son. Well, may be every dad says that but I'm dying and I won't say things I don't mean."

"I know dad. But you're not dying, not yet."

They both looked relax. As if nothing had happened. As if they were talking about the most ordinary things in life, yet they were facing the life's bitter truth.

"Death is a strange thing, isn't it? The most blatant truth of life, yet everybody wants to escape it as long as possible." Will said philosophically. It had been a long time since they had spoken to each other.

"Do you want to escape?" Reeve explored.

Will laughed and replied. "Some things in life are beyond human control my son?"

"And some things aren't." Reeve had a determined answer.

"Do you wanna try?" Will asked in a casual mood.

"If you don't mind."

"Perhaps, I don't have enough time to mind for anything but if you think you've some magic, go ahead. Be my guest, as they say."

Reeve took out an instrument from his box. It had long flexible pipes.

"Oh! You've got something for me?" His dad reacted.

"This is Endoscope. I would need some cells from your pancreas and that's it for now."

He put one end of the pipe down under his throat and within fifteen minutes of efforts he managed to collect some cells.

Next day he sent the cells to the laboratory for testing. By the evening the results were on his table. He opened the envelope and read the report. The results were surprising. Will had a rare type of exocrine pancreatic cancer called Cystic cancer. Almost ninety five percent of pancreatic cancers were incurable but this was in the remaining five percent. He went to see his dad in the evening.

"So what's your guess? How many days are left for me?"

"I don't know. May be five years, may be ten or may be longer, I don't know."

"So what's that magic that you seem to have stretched six month to five years or beyond?"

"If I can say so, there is never a magic but always a reality. Inability to see that reality is what you call magic. In your case, reality is that you've a very rare form of pancreatic cancer which we is going to cured by surgery." Reeve explained.

"Didn't I say that I'm proud of you my son?" Will said happily.

Within two weeks, a surgery was performed to remove his cancer and he was healthier as ever.

17. A Game Of Chess

10th December' 1995.

The guests were surprised to see the birthday cake. They had never seen anything weird like that. They had seen children demanding for all sorts of things they wanted as the shape of their cake but not that! It was a cake in the shape of a pair of kidneys in reddish brown colour, almost the same colour as the real kidneys. When Helen had asked Tracey that what shape she wanted that year on her cake? She had replied after a bit of thought, "I think I want to go for a kidney shape cake and not one but two big kidneys please! What if, I've got only one kidney but I can always have two kidneys on my cake, can't I, mom?

"Yes, of course love but are you sure about this? You can have a nice pony or even sponge bob on your cake if you like."

"No mom, please, I've decided. It's all about kidneys at the moment in my life and I want is, to have one good fun with kidneys on my birthday."

"As you like my dear, I've no issue." And Helen had printed a 3D image of a kidney from the internet to give it to a bakery shop to show them the shape and colour of the cake.

Everyone wore a birthday cap as if it was mandatory. Tracey wore a birthday princess tiara which Judy had brought for her. The balloons were all over the place. The foil banners with birthday greetings covered walls of the room. A musical candle lit on the table and a glittery 8 shape candle lit on the cake as that day she had just turned 'Eight'. Thankfully she was celebrating it at home, twice in a row, unlike some of her other birthdays which she celebrated in a hospital room. But that was perhaps no relief for her as her condition had only deteriorated drastically since then; but it was not the time to bother about that either because the time was limited in her life and priorities must be set right. There she cut the cake and blew the candles. Everyone started singing the birthday song and few kids got busy bursting the balloons and then came the turn of party poppers with the popping sounds and the colourful confetti spreads around. There were around ten kids who were singing and dancing along to the latest party tunes and doing all sort of mischief while enjoying the refreshments available with plenty of sweets and snacks.

The atmosphere was alive and so were the spirits of the kids as well as of the adults.

For these kids, it was only about that day. They didn't have to plan for their future like super intelligent adults and they didn't keep troubled past inside their mind like sharp minded adults, as they had short memories and perhaps that is why they say that childhood is the best time to enjoy. They ought to make most of what life had to offer then. Next day is not there yet, next day may not come for someone.

It was 10 pm and all the kids and guests had gone by then. Helen checked Tracey's blood pressure from the digital monitor and it gave a reading which seemed to be higher than normal. Helen knew well what range was safe or unsafe and if she needed an extra medicine to control it. She even knew the scientific names of these two ranges of the BP and it was not only because the additional medical knowledge helped her understand things better for herself but also because she knew that Tracey's ever so curious mind could shoot numerous questions at any time about anything. Perhaps she easily could have diverted her, for all the medical questions, to her dad but she preferred to satisfy all her curiosity herself. Tracey had asked about these readings a long back when she was reading her medical file. "Mom, why there are two readings for BP?" "Good question! Our heart circulates the blood to all over the body and in order to circulate this blood it maintains some pressure or force on the walls of blood vessels. When the blood leaves the heart through arteries it has the highest blood pressure, and that is the first reading you can see that is higher than the other one. And as the blood moves through the arteries, arterioles, capillaries and veins, the pressure drops and the pressure at the end of this cycle is the minimum pressure which is the second reading, lower than the first one." Helen had felt proud that she was probably able to explain it but it didn't last long.

"And is there any name for these two different readings?"

Helen was caught off guard and she couldn't answer that but promised to find out and tell her if there were any names. Later she found out that there were indeed medical terms as the higher value is termed as 'Systolic' and the lower value termed as 'Diastolic'.

Tracey's blood pressure had been swinging up and down for few days and so was her mood. Whenever her BP was high, she felt miserable and felt as if it was not her body but she was wearing a thick grumpy piece of cloth. She was on ACE inhibitors for couple of years but that seemed to be making no effect at times. Helen remembered how silly she had felt when Dr. Patil had told her that Tracey would be on ACE inhibitor and she had asked him, "So how many days she has to stay in the hospital?"

"She doesn't need to stay in the hospital." Dr. Patil said.

"So is this a small piece of kit, we can use at home? She probed further. "

Then Dr. Patil had realized that it had sounded like an equipment to her. "No, no! This is not a machine. ACE stands for angiotensin converting enzyme and ACE inhibitors is a group of drugs that are used primarily to lower blood pressure." But that was two years back and then of course she knows a whole lot about them as gaining medical knowledge had become a part of her life.

The next day she had to take Tracey hospital for her regular dialysis session. Helen was shocked when the expected had come unexpectedly about six months ago. Dr Patil had diagnosed after a series of numerous tests and told that Tracey's kidney problem was at last stage and dialysis was the only way forward for the treatment of ESRD at the moment. End Stage Renal Disease, that's what ESRD stands for, he had told Helen.

"The amount of proteins present in her urine, the glomerular filtration rate test and the other symptoms like high blood pressure, weight loss, weakness etc. clearly indicate that her kidneys functions are negligible at this stage. Dialysis is the process done to replace some of the kidney functioning." Tracey's nephrologists, Dr Patil had explained in a subtle tone while walking around his table. Tracey was more than a patient for him but he didn't want to be more sympathetic than Helen's pride could take. Helen was one of the strongest person he had ever met.

He had continued, "There are two types of dialysis processes. One is called Haemodialysis and the other one is called peritoneal dialysis and I'll explain you later in detail about this but in short both are effective. As far as patient is concerned the major difference between them is that while peritoneal dialysis can be done at home by patient on their own, the haemodialysis is usually done in a dialysis unit in hospital. Also haemodialysis may be performed 3 times a week for couple of hours in each session but the peritoneal dialysis needs to be done 3-4 times daily." And the explanations and advices had continued in the next few sessions of appointments and follow up appointments in which they had tried to explain all the aspects about the dialysis and the options available for Tracey. As if going through the mental stress of dialysis was not enough pain for the little Tracey, Dr Patil had also told her that for dialysis access she would need an AV fistula which required a small surgery on her arm, preferably in non-dominant arm, to create a fistula by joining an artery and vein to receive the dialysis. Although the other options to gain access to the blood for dialysis were an intravenous catheter or a synthetic graft, Dr. Patil had strongly recommended for AV fistula and Helen knew she could rely on him. It could take few months to her fistula to develop before the first session of dialysis may be started, Dr. Patil had advised. Tracey was already taking the IV treatment for her iron deficiency in which she had to take the drip by inserting a needle in her arm and then this surgery would only add to her despair.

Doctors have done their part by explaining everything but what am I going to tell Tracey? She had thought. Her mind was working overtime these days. She had to perform a balancing act by being normal at home and trying to make a pleasant atmosphere for Tracey as far as possible so that she doesn't feel the gravity of the circumstances. After all she is only eight – how she is going to understand all this? She ought to enjoy this time of her life, she thought. But then again, her child's life was on stake and that was the only constant thing on her mind and yet she had to laugh at times to make her child laugh.

She wondered how her little body was going to cope with all that pain and eternal misery. The scars left on her various parts of the body, by various surgeries and frequent skin problems due to side effects of her illness and drugs were ever increasing. At times her whole body system seemed to had been falling apart. She was anaemic with high blood pressure and the drugs she was taking got her rashes all over her body. She felt weak and dull. High body temperatures made matters worse and the cold and cough topped on that. The ever present danger of failing kidney function was by default and seemed like a thing not to be counted. She was getting various infections regularly due to her weak immune system. At times, Helen was overwhelmed and so were Tracey and Judy. After seeing them, "perhaps, 'overwhelming' was an inadequate word", the language experts sitting at Oxford would have thought. Her body seemed to be welcoming all sorts of diseases and she had to take a heap of medicines in an attempt to rescue herself. Her room was filling more rapidly with medicines than any other thing. A couple of chest and drawers which once upon a time belonged to her toys and stuff were gloomily exhibiting the bottles and wrappers of drugs. Even a child like her with a maturity higher than her age has had her odd days when she refused to take medicine on schedule.

"Mom, I just can't have any medicine now. I'll be sick if I take any." Tracey had told her, she was really miserable that day.

"Tracey, you want to get better soon, don't you?" Helen argued although she felt sick at stomach saying that because it wasn't entirely true.

"Yes mom, but you know for how long I've been taking these drugs but my health is getting worse rather than any recovery so even if I miss once I won't die, would I?.

"Tracey, don't you ever say it again. Please. Nothing will happen to you, OK. Now, you don't want to go to hospital again, do you?" Helen had insisted although she could feel her misery. This is just not fair - she is less than nine years old and all these diet restrictions and being chased for medicines, three-four times a day is not an easy thing to comprehend sometimes for her. She pondered.

"Please mom, please!" she pleaded.

Helen had to give up but it was a two edge sword. If she didn't have medicine on time, it may had worsen her condition and if she forced her to take then it'll a bit rude to her, and in her condition she wanted to make her happy in whatever way possible she could.

Helen was getting ready to go with Tracey for her dialysis appointment at 11am. Though Reeve had suggested to take Tracey with her as dialysis unit was in his hospital itself but Helen knew, he won't be able to sit with her for hours during full dialysis session because of his work commitments, so she decided to go with her on each session. She wanted to be with her all the time during dialysis. "Shall we move now?" She asked Tracey.

"I guess so, mom, I wish you ask me this to go somewhere better than hospital."

Helen came closer to her and sat on knees to hold her and hugged her, "My darling! I know! But have faith; one day everything will be alright. Let's move now." She marvelled at people who don't have time to go with children for a family outing because of their work or because of their lives were too busy to spend some quality time with their children and here, she had almost given up her business to meet Tracey's growing medical needs. Although, Judy was taking care of her horses and the business side as much as she could, Helen managed to visit her farms on weekends sometimes. She wondered how she would have managed everything without Judy. If she was the life support for Tracey then Judy was for her.

They reached children's dialysis unit just before 11am. It was in a big area, beautifully decorated with children's theme and had quite a lot of toys and play items for different age groups. If all the medical equipment and drugs were taken out of this place it could have attracted a lot of parents to come here for entertainment but that was not the case. Perhaps there was something in the air which made children cry a lot there and not feel attracted to all the toys and stuff, as if they knew that despite the atmosphere being so attractive and beautiful, they didn't belong there. Within a few minutes, Tracey was sitting on a reclining medical chair that was specially made comfy for hours of sitting as dialysis was a few hours process, depending upon the size, age and other factors of the patient. The dialysis machine was on Tracey's left side. Helen sat on a chair on her right side. The nurse, Debbie, inserted two needles into her AV fistula which was in her left arm, one to carry blood to the dialyser and another to return the filtered blood to her body. The process was to last around two hours. "So, do you want to play chess again, angel?" Debbie asked Tracey. Angel - that is what she always called Tracey since she met her first time. "Let me tell you, you're very lucky to be the mother of such a wonderful, intelligent, and funny child. God! I just can't help stop adoring her." A truly overwhelmed Debbie had told Helen. But it was not the first time Helen had seen such a reaction. There was a charisma in her which seems to have charmed everyone she met. It was beyond her divine innocence, quick wit or funny tricks she always managed to do. It was the joy people felt inside; it was the enlightenment people sensed from her character.

"Yes, please. You know Debbie; I must have to go to heaven after I die." Tracey replied.

"Oh! You surely will go to heaven but not so soon. Why do you say so?" Her nurse, Debbie asked.

"Because you're surely going to go to heaven after doing so much good deed to me and I've to go there to repay you because I won't be able to repay you for all that in this life, would I? Tracey explained.

"You cheeky little angel." Debbie reacted and placed a table above her leg for the chessboard. "There you go."

"Now, tell me who is the angel? It's you Debbie." Tracey said softly. Debbie hugged her fourth time since she arrived that day. It was as if she felt calmed after hugging a holy figure. Tracey then addressed to her mom, "Mom, today, I'm gonna win all the games".

After the surgery was done on Tracey for AV fistula, Dr. Patil had told Helen that fistula may take months to develop for the dialysis. She had used those months to teach Tracey to play chess as it was an instant time killer. Then they would play chess without realizing the time and hours would go by easily.

They usually had enough time to play one or two games depending upon how a game took shape.

"Let's see, yesterday I managed to win one game but I might win both today." Helen said. She was only as good as Tracey as she had learned it from Reeve just before she started coaching Tracey. At home, they even forged an alliance to win against Reeve, the strongest player among the three of them. Sometimes Reeve offered them to change the side in middle of the game when their alliance was losing a game badly. It was not out of pity to let them win but a smart tactic to create his own interest in the game. It also gave the weak opponent much needed boost and in turn put the life back in an otherwise one sided losing game.

The great game of mind was going on intensely when nurse Debbie broke the eerie silence. "We're done now. But there is no appointment until next one hour so I've no problem if you continue as long as you tell me that my Angel is winning."

"Yes I'm winning, I'm winning." Tracey replied hastily.

"No way! You aren't winning this but we can agree on a draw here." Helen corrected her smilingly. "Well, I can't leave this game just because you're winning, can I? Beside, haven't you told me that one must not lose the hope? I may still win this game; it's not finished yet, is it?" Tracey replied.

Helen wondered, if that was true in her life as well, if only there was a slim hope that her health would improve over the years but doctors had shown her the graph which only went downwards. "I won't give you a false hope. Kidney functioning will only get worse in coming years; she'll need dialysis and then eventually a transplant." Dr. Patil had told her. And Helen knew that even a transplant may not last forever.

Despite having all the pessimistic views about Tracey's health, Helen left the dialysis centre that day with a new sense of courage and dignity that were missing uncharacteristically for quite a few days.

18. Brother And Business

"Dr. Harvey, do you accept that you failed to obtain informed consent of the patient to perform the surgery as per the regulations of the medical board of the Globe hospital." One of the five members of the panel present asked at a disciplinary hearing against Reeve.

"Yes, I do."

"Can you explain us why?"

"I'm sure everybody present here knows why."

"We would like to hear from you."

"My patient Mrs. Robinson was 18 weeks pregnant when she came in with the stomach pain. Further investigation and tests revealed that there was an infection caused by the foetus. The infection was spreading rapidly in her body and the survival chance of patient was less than five percent without removing the foetus. I had taken the decision to remove the foetus."

"But Mrs. Robinson did not approve that surgery, did she?"

"No, she did not because she was worried that it might be her last chance to have her own child."

"Why did you not approve her concern then?"

"She was only 35. What if, she had a miscarriage earlier! She was healthy enough for me to believe that she can be pregnant again. Even if she can't be pregnant, there are other artificial ways to have a child. Adoption is another way of having children. Having said that, this question would have never rose if she was not alive, would it? Being a doctor, I have taken the decision with my full conscious and mind, keeping emotions at bay.

What my patient was asking was a 'suicide', without a justifiable reason. This country doesn't approve of suicide and I am sure neither do any of you present here. I'm a doctor, by choice, and I'll save a life as long as I can, without worrying about the outcome of this committee."

The committee had left him with a warning but that was not the first time he had come before disciplinary committee of the Globe hospital. He was called before the committee for the smallest of issues which was driven by a constant urge of some of his colleagues to frame him in, and get him suspended. Once, he was being investigated for not wearing gloves for a few minutes when he examined a patient's eyes in the operation room. In other case, he was being questioned when a little girl wanted to gift him a 'tie' after the full recovery of her surgery and her parents had requested Reeve to accept it but somebody present there had made a big fuss out of that. There were a few senior colleagues of him who were threatened by Dr. Beckman's ever increasing trust on Reeve and they used their pet staff to spy on Reeve. Dr. Beckman would have finished the matter by just making a call but he was a true professional and never interfered in any routine procedures of the hospital. He had told Reeve, before the committee meeting, "I won't ask you anything and I know you don't want to tell me anything either, but I know you're clean. Go to the committee. I won't take any side or express any opinion before committee as I'm sure our hospital has an efficient committee to look into these issues. It will only do justice, and will take every aspect of the enquiry into concern."

For Dr. Beckman and Reeve business was as usual.

"There is no dearth of whistle-blowers to come against you, Reeve, is there? Joe had once chuckled with Reeve.

After the hearing, Dr. Patil and Joe had come in his room. "Can't you see they are spying on you Reeve? It's just a personal vendetta of Dr. James, isn't it?" Dr. Patil warned him.

"I don't need to see what they're doing. How does it matter to me if they are spying on me when I'm not doing anything wrong?" Reeve replied calmly.

"But this is not about you doing 'anything wrong'; they are implicating you by presenting things in immoral ways. Did you not hear they called you incompetent and insincere?"

"Don't worry. I've been called worse." Reeve remained calm.

"What's the matter with you Reeve? It may have got you suspended or your licence might have been revoked." Dr. Patil said passionately. He looked clearly provoked then.

"Don't worry, it won't be so soon." Reeve assured him further.

"But why can't you come openly and slam the people who are trying to malign your reputation?"

"I don't care what they say; my reputation is my patients"

"Gordon Bennett!! Tell him somebody."

"Hey Patil, have you read bible?" Joe, who was hearing the conversation quietly chipped in.

"What is it about bible?" Dr. Patil got even more irritated.

"In Bible, it says, 'love thy enemies'. So our Reeve is a saint, don't try to tell him otherwise." Joe tried to put some humour into the situation, for he knew advice were no good to Reeve anyway.

"Hello, I'm Jim Harvey from 'Surgimagic' – I've spoken to you on phone." Jim shook hands and introduced himself to the purchase manager, Mark Wolsky, of the Globe hospital. He had carefully planned everything in advance.

"Yes, indeed you had. How can I forget Dr. Reeve's brother? Have a seat Jim." Mark had tremendous respect for Reeve from what he had heard about him although he seldom got a chance to speak to him. If a few people were doing their best to get Reeve down, there were even more people who admired him.

"As I explained to you earlier, my company has already applied a tender for this year's hospital supply and I would be happy, if you can see that through please. Reeve has had a look on product line and he was quite satisfied with that. Can I have a quick chat with him please, just to let him know that I'm here?" Jim said in a breath.

"Yes, sure. Go ahead." Mark pushed the phone towards Jim.

Jim dialled Reeve's number and put the speaker phone 'on', purposefully. He soon heard the voice of Reeve.

"Hi Reeve, this is Jim. I've come to Globe hospital to meet Mark in purchase. Well, you know the reason already why I'm here, so I just thought to let you know."

"Yes, sure. Good luck."

"Thanks. I'll see you after meeting."

"Don't bother Jim? If you want to see me, I'll come to your place in the evening."

"Alright then! Bye." He ended the call and addressed to Mark, "My brother! He loves us so much."

"Yes, of course." Mark replied.

Jim explained all the marketing gimmicks to Mark and said, "You've to consider the quality of our products as well, before taking a decision based on prices. And of course, you can talk to Reeve about the quality of the products. He has seen almost all the products."

"No, that won't be needed. Your word is enough for me." Mark assured him.

Mark had never spoken to Reeve about the tender and Reeve never knew about the talk but the tender was passed within a month of that conversation took place. Jim obliged by throwing a party to celebrate his success. "I've done it! I've done it! WITHOUT your help Reeve." He had mocked at Reeve in the party.

Following his company's contract for medical supply, Jim had to visit the hospital several times on official tours but his big mouth never hesitated in advertising indiscriminately about his relationship with Reeve. Soon Reeve's enemies had another chance to get into action and damage his reputation. "This will nail the bastard." Dr. James had expressed himself to his associate. They demanded a probe to see if Reeve had influenced the decision to give the contract to Jim's company. Jim's contract was cancelled soon and an enquiry was set up to probe the allegations. Perhaps, Jim was his own worst enemy. Mark was shocked to found out that Reeve had not seen any of Jim's products and neither did he have any opinion about them.

19. Joe's Joy

"Dr. Joe an emergency has come with several complications; she is in the ICU in critical condition", nurse Frieda came running and shouted from a few feet distance to Joe who was checking on a patient's file.

"Alright, what is this about?" Joe stood up in an alert manner.

"Her name is Shirley and she is sufferriii-…." Frieda tried to explain.

"What did you say – Shirley?", He demanded before she could finish. His heart was beating faster.

"Yes, Shirley Watson", she replied and was surprised to see the eagerness in his eyes and face.

His heart started pounding. Is she really my Shirley? What happened to her? Where she has been all these bloody days? I can't believe if this is real - the thought of clashing emotions started dancing in his mind in those split seconds, before he asked "And what is the case?

"She is suffering from MS - advance stage", she replied slowly.

He raced towards the ICU to see the patient. The distance from his room to the ICU was barely 50 meter but he wished to fly. He was shocked on his eagerness to expect her in the ICU even after all these years. It had been almost eleven years since he last met her and since then the bitterness towards her was compelling. The feelings of frustration, sadness and betrayal were still alive. Many times in the past, he had tried to console himself by thinking that there must have been some good reason for her to leave him in the way she did; but in the end, he couldn't accept that he could not be trusted to tell the reason whatsoever that was. But whatever it was, he was then entrusted with a unique duty that tied him with the prime relationship of doctor and patient. Everything else mattered least. He entered the ICU room where a few doctors were already treating the patient. He still couldn't see the face of the patient. He juggled around his way between the doctors and tried to peek upon the bed. He was horrified. He took a long and hard look at her. It was his Shirley. Her body looked pale and fragile. He quickly took account of the situation and started assisting in her treatment. After a while, her condition settled down a bit but she was still under the influence of anesthesia. He sat beside her on a chair monitoring her vital signs while realizing that whatever she had caused him – the immense pain and suffering without an apparent reason – he cannot see her suffer, he couldn't see her lying in a bed, suffering from MS. His heart was crying on her suffering. *She should be respected and cared, not for her betrayal but for the love I have for her*, he thought. She was still a part of him. They still belonged to each other like a body and its soul. A body is nothing without a soul, but when somebody dies, we still care it; respect it, and prepare a beautiful coffin for the body which belonged to a soul that has been deserted by the body.

He continued staring at her with a sense of restlessness while going down the memory lane many years back. How he had met her and how she had changed his lives in so many ways. In his mind he could still hear those explosions of laughter they have had together. He remembered his first date and their first dinner together. He remembered every beautiful thing they had done together in those two years of courtship. He remembered the great understanding they had together and how their lives seem to be complimenting each other in every respect. He never in a million years would have imagined that their relationship was going to end so abruptly. He remembered the day when he had proposed her and the 'shock of his life' he had received that fateful day.

Then suddenly something else came to his mind which hit him hard. In the fury of those moments, when the team of doctors was treating her in the emergency, somebody had told him that the patient was suffering from MS for past twelve years. Multiple Sclerosis – that must have been the reason Shirley has left me. He was overwhelmed with guilt and pain. Everything was becoming so clear to him. Everything she did, everything she made up or tried to hide. Every word she had said in their last meeting was making sense to him. "I love you and I always will. A marriage is unjust without love; a marriage is a betrayal without love. But a love is neither unjust nor betrayal without marriage. And I love you and I always will. But in a marriage I have to make some commitments; commitment to make our life happy and satisfied; commitment to help you and be with you when you chase our dreams; commitment to make you feel special in the same way I will be for you; commitment to be truthful and to be able to gain your trust and confidence. And I don't think I am ready for this. For this reason I must not accept this. I am indebted to you for asking me to marry you, but I am equally hurtful for the pain my words may cause to you".

She had started waking up then. Joe was still sitting beside her. She opened her eyes slowly and tried to make sense of her surroundings. She was brought in the hospital in an unconscious state and didn't know where she was. She moved her face to see on her right side and found that somebody was looking at her intently. That somebody looked familiar to her. She looked again – this time more closely. She mumbled, "Joe?"

"Yes, darling!" He whispered. He couldn't control then. They were tears of pure joy; of pure peace; of pure lightness he felt in his heart. The heaviness; the sense of loss; the frustration; the mystery he had for all those years were all gone.

"Joe!" She called again in a much louder voice. The euphoria was beginning to engulf both of them. They hugged each other as hard as they could. It was a day when only love had won – overcoming destiny, disease and the entire predicament that comes with this world.

Within a couple of days, she had made recovery and most of her symptoms were gone, at least for then. Joe had finished all his work and came to see her. She was sitting on her bed and looked happy. "I was just waiting for you." She said.

"I know that's why I've come as soon as I could." He replied.

"I feel sorry."

"Sorry for what?"

"I feel sorry that you would have forgotten me completely in all these years and now here I've met you again by chance."

"Forgotten you? How COULD I? What kind of love I have had for you, if I could ever forget you? Every day and every night of these 11 years I have thought about you. Every morning I've woken up with you on my mind, and every night I have slept with dreaming about you. And you think I've forgotten you? Did YOU forget me in all these years?"

She waited for a few seconds before replied, "I haven't. How could I? I've always loved you. I've loved you for my life."

"No, you didn't! If you had, then you would have trusted me to tell everything. You would've known that I loved you as much you loved me. You would've known that my love will remain same for you for better or worse of times." He said with a tone of shouting; of crying; of pleading.

She looked down, not as if, she felt guilty but as if, it was the only way to recognize his love; his pain. After a few seconds, she moved her lips, "I knew how much you loved me and I know how much you love me even now. But to suffer in pain without you and your love was my love to you. To miss you every day and night was my love to you. To give you a chance to forget me and start a fresh life without me was my love to you. To save you from seeing me physically suffering was my love to you. To give you freedom from someone who could not even talk, walk or do anything at times, was my love to you. How could I've destroyed your life when I, a patient of MS, knew well what I was going through that time? Do you remember when we went to Saltburn and I denied a walk along the beach - my legs were so numb that I could barely stand? Do you remember the day when we were having a candle light dinner and I insisted you to leave in a hurry because I was so dizzy and knew that an attack was imminent. Do you know how many times I'd avoided you on the phone because my speech was blurred? Do you know how many times I'd to take my hand back from you holding it, because I felt clumsiness in my hands due to this evil MS? Do you know how many times I'd to cancel our date because of those MS related relapses? I couldn't see how I could have brought any happiness when I was physically so challenged.

Do you think it was easy for me to deny marrying you? That was all I ever wished, I ever wanted in my life – to MARRY YOU!! I had already thought about this before even you offered me to marry. After marriage, what would I have offered you except asking for your help all the time? A nice talk, when my speech was so blurred? A nice company when my hands and feet were so numb? A nice outing with you, when I felt so droopy? Or a nice food, when I couldn't even open a bloody jar with my bare hands? At times my energy levels were so low that I couldn't even take a glass of water for myself. My relapses were becoming so frequent that I didn't know how fast and how much it's going to be worse. I wanted to tell you everything before I leave you but then I knew you wouldn't let me go and in one way it made sense to me that the more you'll hate me, the more it'll be easy for you to forget me. I never thought, we'll meet again but then I underestimated the destiny and here we go, sitting together, as if we were never separated."

The power of love had never been so evident. Whilst Joe was hearing her side of the story, at the same time the bitterness he had for her for the last eleven years was melting away, as if it never existed. It was a kind of love that had a protective coating of bitterness but that was not required anymore. Love was the only bonding meant to exist between them. The gush of emotions were freely flowing through their heart, mind and body like pure water that flows through the massive Niagara Falls.

"Shirley! I never thought you were so selfish! I thought you believed in sharing. All these years, you endured my share of pain and even love. How could you think that I'll forget you so easily if you suddenly decides to disappear from my life? How could you think that I can ever be happy without you? How could you think that you'll destroy my life, no matter in what physically challenged condition you were? Do you think I've lived all these years without you? No – there wasn't a life without you for me. Trust me! I wouldn't have a slightest of doubt in giving up a million years of my life without you for even a single year of life with you.

You taught me to love and you doubted my love? I've loved you with all my heart. Nobody, nothing, could have ever replaced, my love for you. Even if, you could not talk to me, silence is enough for us; if, you could not go out with me; your company is enough for me; if, you could not do anything for me, the mere knowledge is enough that you love and care for me? I would have been much more happy just by seeing you beside me rather than suffering without you. I would have done everything for you without any expectation or without even realizing what I was doing for you because, that is the power of love and when you love somebody nothing matters for you except the company of somebody you love.

Do you remember you once said that If you love somebody for one and only reason and expectation – love - that is some form of love and if you get the same love in return. That is the only final form of love. I thought our love was the 'final form of love' – wasn't it? Wasn't it?" Joe repeated in a husky voice.

Tears were pouring down from Shirley's eyes as if she had saved them for years for that moment. "Yes I had said that, and yes I never doubted your love but I also said that anything less, anything more will impure it, and maybe I wasn't sure of myself, I was scared of the impurity of kindness in our love. Yes, I was wrong. I was so wrong! Even after all those years, we are, what we were to each other, when I left you, and we always will, no matter what happens in the future."

Joe took her right hand in his right hand and said, "They say history repeat itself, and today, history WILL repeat itself but I hope not ALL but some - only some part of it." He bowed down on his knees once again in his life and asked her, "Will you marry me?"

"YES, I'll! YES! YES! YES!" Shirley said in an exhilarating voice.

The very next day, a meeting room of that same hospital was converted into a marriage ceremony hall and a gathering was arranged. Helen attended as her best maid and Reeve as his best mate. Shirley sat on a chair while minister asked Joe to take his marriage vows. He took Shirley's right hand and in his left hand and repeated after minister, "I, Joe Ferguson, take you Shirley Watson, to be my lawfully wedded wife; and I do promise................in joy and in sorrow; in sickness and in health; as long as we shall live together."

Minister asked her, if she could stand up and take her vows, she felt as if she was stuck to the seat and couldn't get up but before she could say anything, Joe picked her up in his arms and indicates minister to proceed. Shirley repeats after the minister, "I, Shirley Watson, take you Joe Ferguson, to be my lawfully wedded husband........."

20. Waiting List

"Hurry up sweetheart! Your dad is getting late for work." Helen primed Tracey who had yet not finished her breakfast. She was a slow eater like her granny.

"Mom, I just don't feel like eating anything. Can I put this in the fridge and finish it when I'm back? Tracey said to her mom, her plate was still almost full of different fruit portions. It was yet another appointment for her but it was not a routine dialysis but a special one. Today she was called for a kidney transplant assessment. She had gone through several tests in last few weeks that included urine test, certain virus infection test such as hepatitis etc., tissue type test, chest X-ray and many more. Helen had started noting all the labs and their results in a diary but two years back she had given up. *It's no good noting them down*, she had decided. She had now lost the count how many times these tests had been done over and over again in the last eight years.

"It's alright. I'll put in the fridge. You go up, put on your shoes and we're up and ready to go!" Helen replied.

"Thanks mom." And off she went to pick her shoes.

"I suppose you've kept all the reports in this bag, right?" Reeve asked from the front room which was adjacent to the dining room. Helen had kept a leather bag on the table in which she usually collected all medical reports of Tracey.

"Yes. I'm coming in a sec." Helen shouted from the kitchen. They were going together as Tracey's appointment was almost the same time as Reeve's working time.

After about forty minutes of drive, Helen parked the car in a large parking area of the transplant building of the Globe hospital. The transplant building bore the name 'Ben's Life

Pulses', which was named after the pioneer surgeon of Globe Hospital, Ben Timothy, who died of a heart stroke just after performing a life-saving operation. Like the main building, this building was also surrounded by a huge garden which had many art pieces. Reeve had performed many heart transplant surgeries in that building in last three years and then that day, her own daughter was going to be evaluated for a transplant. It was one of the most advanced transplant centre where five-ways kidney transplant could take place simultaneously. "But why we'll need five transplants at a same time anyway? Helen had asked in a Transplant information session when she was told about that.

"Very good question, why we would need that? Sometimes, in a group of patients who have wiling donor available– usually a family member or a friend – but recipient is not the exact match for the transplant but it matches another in the group. The operations are performed at the same time so that willing donors do not change their mind once their own family member or a friend has received the kidney from another donor in that group." Mr. Hudson had explained.

Reeve left the reception area in a hurry to start his work, leaving Tracey and Helen to meet with the transplant co-ordinator. Within fifteen minutes, a young lady, who appeared to be in her twenties came to see them and introduced herself. "Hello, I'm Melissa Scott and I guess you're Tracey? I'm your transplant coordinator."

Helen and Tracey introduced themselves with a sense of uncertainty in the air. Helen would have liked Reeve to be with her but that day he had urgent appointments to keep but he had promised to catch up as soon as possible.

"Would you like to come with me, and then we can start the process?"

Helen nodded and followed her in a gallery to reach in a small room.

"Have a seat please. Would you like some tea, coffee?"

"We're fine but thank you for asking." Helen replied on behalf of herself and Tracey.

"Tracey, would you like some juice or any drink?" Melissa insisted. Helen got a feeling that she was just trying to be extra polite to make things easy but no matter how hard she was trying, it wasn't easy for Helen – not then. Since last couple of days, Helen's mind had a storm of questions about transplant, even though Reeve had already explained her in detail the next steps in getting the transplant done.

"I need some information from you to fill up some forms and then I'll explain you step by step everything involved with the transplant. Is that OK?" Melissa asked.

It took them around an hour to fill up the forms. It was not just the usual details she was interested in, like name or address but every minute details of Tracey's last eight years of medical history. Then she explained that once the evaluation process is successfully completed, Tracey would be listed on a local and national computerized database which would then allocate a kidney based on several factors like blood group, tissue matching, age etc.

"How soon she might expect?" Helen probed further.

"It's really difficult to say children do get priority over others but it really depends upon tissue type, blood match and other factors like waiting list and availability of donors. At an average it may take from one year to three years. But as I said, if you would be able to arrange for a living donor then you don't have to wait." Melissa tried to explain her. The answer was simple and plain – they just had to wait and watch. *That is what I've been doing for last eight years, waiting for some good news, for a way out that would show me some positive hope into Tracey's future,* she thought. And yet again, Melissa had added a few more years in her eternal wait.

It was evening when they finished their meetings with various people involved in transplant evaluation. Helen called Reeve after Melissa had told her that they could leave then, "We've just finished now, what about you?"

"I can leave in another half an hour."

"OK, we'll wait in the café." Reeve joined them within half an hour and they left for the car park to go back home. "Hmm. It must be tiring I suppose." Reeve enquired.

"Yes, at least for Tracey." Helen agreed.

"I'm fine. Fair to middle." Tracey humoured.

"You're a brave girl, aren't you?" Reeve gave her a brief smile while driving.

"I've got the confirm dates for Tracey to have dialysis in Benidorm." Helen said to Reeve while serving rice to Reeve on dinner table. Tracey's dialysis co-ordinator Elaine had helped her find a suitable dialysis unit and organize for Tracey to have dialysis during a week's holidays they had planned. She then had to have dialysis for three hours, three times a week. Helen had been planning for that holiday for the last few weeks. She marvelled at people who could simply go to their nearest travel agent and choose their best destination while she had to arrange for the medical facilities first and then only she could think about other leisurely activities. That was the right time for a holiday or rather it was the only time to go on a holiday in a foreseeable future as Tracey was preparing for her transplant and once transplant formalities were completed, she wouldn't want to go anywhere and miss her opportunity of getting a transplant. Even after transplant she would need some care before she could be out on a holiday.

"Good! Have you completed the formalities for medical facilities there?"

"Yes, there were mainly two forms to fill in – P10 and E111 for medical facilities there."

"Excellent. You haven't booked the tickets yet, have you?"

"No, I haven't even done the hotel bookings yet. I wanted to tell you first."

"Thanks! Give me the dates; I'll check my schedule and let you know tomorrow."

"I'll", she then addressed to Tracey, who was munching noodles – a treat she was getting after days of strict diet, "Tracey – are you not excited about the holidays?"

"No, I'm very much. Is nana coming with us?" Tracey replied cheerfully.

"She is, darling, don't worry." Helen assured her. Judy wasn't interested to go on holidays and leave her horses behind for a week but Tracey and Helen had managed to persuade her finally.

"Has it got lots of theme parks 'cause I wanna take lots of ride there?" Tracey asked.

"Yes, certainly. I hope you stay fit and fine."

"I'll mom, besides dad will be there, and he won't let anything happen to me." It was a conviction she had, having her dad as a doctor, but perhaps perceptions were always different then realities.

"I'll try. I'll try." Reeve nodded to Tracey.

The flight landed at Alicante airport at sharp 11am. Benidorm was on northern Costa Blanca coast of Spain and was not far from Alicante. They picked up a taxi outside of arrivals to go to the hotel. Tracey tried her hands on what she had learned in her Spanish classes, to communicate with the taxi driver Emilio. "You're an intelligent girl", Emilio, who was already impressed, had complimented Tracey in Spanish. He also told her about the places she should visit in and around Benidorm. It was a cheerful start for Tracey. Their hotel was on a rather quiet place over viewing the Peacock Island. Helen knew that Benidorm was a busy place but she had planned their itinerary in the way that they got enough time to relax and recover, and at the same time lots of entertainment for Tracey.

After they reached the hotel, there was not much planned for the rest of the day except relaxing, trying local food, get into the holiday mood and a leisurely walk along the Levante beach. They needed to charge their energies for the next day when lots of activities were planned.

On the sixth floor of a tall building of Globe hospital, Dr. Neil Beckman was sitting on an executive leather chair in his chamber. It was a large chamber with huge plain windows reducing the walls to negligible. He looked out from the window - the beautiful gardens, the breath-taking medical sculptures, and a massive fountain in middle of that. An ambulance had just come in and a child came out of it on a stretcher. He knew that a very good care would be taken for that child. He had put the best systems, people and tools in place. But his thoughts were disarrayed that day between his patients and the future of his great hospital. In last 38 years, his hospital had been his life; his family; his children; his relatives and his friends. He had loved every bit of it. The hospital staff had celebrated his 74th birthday just a few weeks ago. But he was then worried about the future of his hospital after him. He urgently needed a succession plan not only for after him, but even for many years to come after that. He was not dying yet but he knew it was daft to try to catch the 'last' coach of a running train. *The death must be creeping in slowly*, he had thought many times so rather leaving things for the last minute, he had already prepared a blueprint of a hospital trust which would take care of everything after him. He felt restless that day. Just half an hour before, he had finished with the board meeting that he had called to discuss on his blue print of succession plans. He badly missed Reeve in the meeting. *He should have been here today,* he thought. He couldn't ask him to stay for this meeting as he knew Reeve and his family more than deserved that holiday. He was feeling even more restless then and his stomach had started aching now. He dialled his home number and called on his wife.

"Hello, Jillian speaking." His wife answered the phone.

"Darling! I missed you. Would you be able to come here right away and be my dearest?"

"Surely, I can, but is everything OK, Neil?"

"Please, don't ask. Have I got any right to be near to you without any reason?

"Oh! I'm flattered Neil, of course you have! I shall come right away." She hung up the phone and hurried to grab the car keys.

His uneasiness was increasing by every passing minute. He wanted to wait for Jillian but he suspected it to be a silent heart attack and called the emergency. Within few minutes he was in one of his 'intensive care unit' where he had operated on numerous patients over the years. The news of Dr. Beckman's stroke had spread in a flash across the hospital staff, doctors and patients. Many people gathered outside of the unit. The uncertainty was in the air.

Neil opened his eyes and found Jillian was sitting next to him. She held his hands and looked deep into his eyes. "Why didn't you tell me? She asked slowly.

"Darling! Would you forgive me for anything that has ever hurt you or for anything that I might not be able to do for you?" Neil whispered while removing his oxygen mask partially.

"Please! You shouldn't be saying this. You'll be alright honey. "

"Darling! I'm a doc' and I can feel. It has come now. I wish I could have seen Reeve, before I can say goodbye."

"Would you like me to give a call to Reeve and tell him?"

"No. No. I wouldn't interrupt their holiday for anything. Promise me to tell him only when he is back, no matter what happens."

"I promise."

She continued, "do you remember when we went to Venice and I slipped while putting my feet into boat and you quickly held my hand and supported me?"

"Yes, yes, I do."

"Do you remember what you said?"

"I can't remember; my poor memory!"

"You said, you won't let me leave so easily, and I always remember it."

They chatted for a few minutes but in the evening Neil had another severe attack and just after six in the evening, he was resting in peace. For many, he was a father figure and for others, he was a messiah, who saved lives and helped people.

Jillian requested everyone to leave her alone for a few minutes with his body. She wanted to be in his company and feel strength, like she always did. She wanted to laugh with him and show all her happiness to him, like she always did. She wanted to hold her emotions back and be strong; instead she cried all her heart out like a child. She forgot her existence; her surrounding; her heart beat; her senses – because her 'world' had died. She felt as if there was no purpose, no courage, and no desire left for her to carry on. Fifty six years of fairy-tale union had come to an end. They say it gets boring when time passed by. You'd be surprised how interesting it gets – when your depth of love and trust consumes all the differences and barriers between you and your partner, and your warmth and dependence on each other only increases by each passing day to melt away the distances between two hearts.

21. Carry On Legacy

Joe called up Reeve as soon as they arrived in a cold and dull morning of London after a week's holiday in sunny Spain.

"Hey Reeve, has it really been a week only! It seems, I'm talking to you after ages. How are things, Tracey? Can we meet this evening?" He shot a series of questions in one go.

"Yes, we can. What time? 6pm or whenever?"

"See you then at 6. Bye."

Joe came in the evening and explained about the sudden and unwelcome event of the week. Helen and Reeve called on Jillian and offered their condolences but she requested them to see her as soon as possible. They promised to come by the same evening and soon, after they had made the call, they left to meet Jillian.

"I was waiting for you all to return from holidays." Jillian said.

"You should have called Jillian." Helen said while holding her hand.

"Neil would have been cross with me, if I had done so."

"Please call us if you ever need."

"I will. Thank you." She replied and walked to the nearest chest of drawers and retrieved an envelope. "That is for you Reeve - from Neil."

"Hmm, do you know what it is?"

"You have to read it. Neil's lawyer, Mr. Dixon will soon make an appointment to see you."

"Hmm."

They left for the home after a brief stay but he didn't open the envelope yet. In the night, after dinner, he opened the envelope in his study room. It was a letter from Neil…

Dear Reeve,

When you're reading this; this will be the only means of communicating with you and me. I would want you to congratulate for being the new owner of the Globe hospital. Sorry! Wrong – I would rather request you to be the 'caretaker' of the Globe hospital, and trusting you would accept it, I've transferred all my shares of hospital in your name and Mr. Dixon should see you soon in this regard.

You, being an intelligent man, would appreciate the fact that I'm neither doing any favors by doing so, nor any charity, but a pure selfish act of protecting 'my interests'. I've realized that you're the only man I could trust; that you're the only person, I believe, can see beyond the materialistic value of 'my interests'; can act beyond the usual boundaries of self-interests; can progress beyond the common horizons of success.

My interest is my hospital; my interest is my patients; my interest is in my staff and every bit of Globe hospital.

I've also put a plan in place to run this hospital in a much longer future where a trust will be created and the recruitment and terms of the trustees will be based upon certain criteria. Mr. Dixon will provide you a sealed packet which contains the details further. However, I've not put a timeline as and when the trust should be created as I believe you running the hospital would be at least as good as me, if not more, so I would request you to act as the 'caretaker' of this hospital, until the trust is up and running.

Give my love to Tracey and Helen. I wish, Tracey receives the transplant soon and live a happy life; she is our hospital's patient; she is my interest – you see.

Best wishes.

Neil Beckman

Reeve put the letter on the desk, sat silently for a couple of hours and then went to sleep. The next day was going to be a busy day.

Everybody in the hospital was waiting for their new boss. Jillian had arranged for a circular to be sent to everyone to inform about it, and with advice that Reeve should not be contacted in that regard before he joined the hospital back after his holiday. When Reeve reached the hospital that morning, few media persons were there to seize the moment in their electronic devices and some threw out their usual flashy questions to him. He excused himself and went in where people were ready to greet him and express their pleasure to have him as their boss. He gracefully accepted their best wishes but made clear that he had not come here as their boss but as a part of a great team. The staff who didn't know him well were in awe of the greatest humility on show. The staff who knew him had already expected that. But for some it was a bad news. Dr. James and others who had conspired against him in the past, had put in their papers. Reeve went to see every one of them personally. "Dr. James, what would you want from me before you throw this paper in the bin?" Reeve said to Dr. James showing his resignation letter.

"I thought that's what you would want from me eventually – my resignation."

"How can I? How - Can - I? You're one of the best Neurologists in the whole UK. The Globe hospital is indebted to you to have saved several lives. Dr. James. We are doctors - not politicians. We save lives and that's the only thing I would ask you to do for our hospital. This hospital needs you – you're one of the best brains we have in this hospital. If anything, you think can be done to improve our facilities; you must come forward and raise your voice. You are as much entitled to do that as anybody else." He paused for a couple of second and added, "There is the bin. Please bin it yourself." Reeve handed over his resignation letter to him.

"But I didn't say 'yes'?"

"I'm prepared to eliminate any reason to say 'no'."

A bronze statue of Dr. Neil Beckman was erected in the front garden of Globe hospital. *It's a temple and only thing missing is its god*, Reeve had thought and decided. Dr. Neil was his mentor and was somehow the only source of inspiration, not only for him but for many, whose lives were touched by his charismatic spirit.

Last six months had been the most challenging and busy times of Reeve's life. He spread out his time efficiently in doing the treatment of patients as well as taking care of administrative side of the hospital. He had the responsibility of taking his hospital to new heights. He focused not on increasing the number of beds but to provide the treatments for those chronic and rare diseases that were either not available in the country or the ones people could not afford to pay. Anybody was entitled to apply for a free treatment but there was a system to check their financial standings and for those who really could not afford, the free services were offered. All the profit from the hospital was either reinvested in getting the new equipment and machines which were rare but essential, or spent on the free treatment of the poor patients. His hospital became the first to go online and publish performance data of his hospital including the death rates considering factors such as diagnosis, risk involved and age.

22. A Girl In Coma

Helen dialed Melissa's number again. It was something she had been doing frequently those days. "Melissa, this is Helen. I was just wondering, if there is any news on Tracey's transplantation yet." She was sick of asking that over and over again.

"No, I'm afraid not yet. You don't need to call me Helen, I shall be calling you immediately as soon as a suitable kidney is available for her. How is Tracey?" And Tracey's transplant coordinator was sick of disappointing her again and again.

"But what if, you aren't available to them to inform about the availability of a kidney?" Helen enquired.

"They have got your number as well; you'll be contacted directly by them. Don't worry about that. You'll be contacted as soon as a kidney is available and keep your pager on, of course, all the time." Melissa assured her once again but perhaps being a bachelor herself, a mother's state of mind was something beyond her understanding. *Goodness, what on earth can I do if a kidney is NOT available,* she murmured in his thoughts. Although, she sympathized with Tracey's condition, there was nothing more she could do about it. She had already advised to arrange for a living donor but nothing had been possible. Tracey's blood type and HLA phenotypes were rare and it couldn't be easily matched.

Unlucky for Tracey, even her own parents, Helen and Reeve were not suitable as a donor for her. Her uncle Dr. Joe had also offered her to donate a kidney but his blood type didn't match either. Judy was a diabetic patient and she could not be operated.

Tracey had blood type 'O' which was a universal donor blood group but it could receive only from blood group 'O' which in turn reduced her chances of matching blood group. Tracey's only hope was a cadaver donor. It had been more than a year then since she was first registered with national transplant list. Helen had planned their holidays just after Tracey's lab tests were done for the transplant assessment, hoping she could get kidney any time after that but even after a year, waiting game was still on. Tracey was ecstatic on prospect of a successful transplant. "Does that mean, I won't be going and sitting for hours in that boring dialysis room?"

"Yes, of course, why would you, when you've received a good kidney?" *Three hours, three times a week, no wonder, you're sick of that place, 'love',* Helen thought and replied.

"That would be great mom! But when will I receive it? You're saying this since we went on holiday."

"I don't know 'love' but it should be soon."

"I want to go on holidays again after that. I had a great time in Benidorm, mom. I think that was the best time I ever had in my life. Thanks again for that mom."

"We all had great time then, didn't we? - you, me, your dad and nana. Don't worry; we'll go again, as soon we get this done."

Reeve clicked his mouse on an icon and it opened the 'critical patients' file on his computer. Patient data in Globe hospital was available online now and they were updated and viewed in real time. Information technology in Globe hospital was one of the Reeve's biggest initiatives, since he took in charge of the hospital. Reviewing the report on 'critical patients' was first thing he did every morning. That day, there were total 4 patients marked as 'critical'. First was a 20 years old girl, Rita, who had a hole in her heart and urgently needed a transplant. Second was a

52 years old lady, Pam, who was suffering from advance stage breast cancer. Third was a 48 years old man, who was a chain smoker and had never heard about COPD and was living with the disease for the last four years. "What does that mean?" He had asked his doctor.

"COPD stands for 'chronic obstructive pulmonary disease'. It's a chronic lung disease..." Dr. Henry then explained him in detail.

Fourth was a 44 years lady, Laney, who was suffering from ESRD and urgently needed a transplant.

He dialed one after another number to speak to his colleague doctors who were responsible for these cases and discussed, case by case. After he finished talking, he looked at his wrist watch – almost an hour was gone, but the day had just begun and that day two transplant operations were scheduled for him.

The fourth case had puzzled him. Dr. Patil who was looking this case had told him that Laney had warned them that if she doesn't get a transplant soon, she would end her life. Her general condition was poor but psychologist, Dr. Aaron Mitchell, had given her a clean chit, so on psychological grounds, she couldn't go up as priority on transplant list and yet she was deemed at risk. Reeve thought for a few minutes and then he had something in his mind. He clicked on an icon again and opened software which could match a given blood and tissue sample with the samples available in hospital database. He entered the blood and tissue data of Laney and ran a search for the matches available. After a few minutes of scanning, computer screen had shown two matches. One was of a patient who had received the transplant in his hospital and second was his own. He remembered, around a year back, his blood and tissue samples were taken to see if he could donate a kidney to Tracey.

He dialled Dr. Patil's number again, "Patil, tell that lady, Laney, that we've found a living donor for her."

"Living donor? Who is that?"

"Not far from you. You're hearing him now."

"I don't get it, is that you?"

"Yes."

"Are you serious?"

"Why? Am I not healthy enough to donate a kidney?"

"No, I don't mean that. You don't know her and why would you take the risk. Also do you understand that you would need some time to recover after that, and you're so busy here?"

"I suppose this is not a prerequisite for a donor to know their recipient well and I don't need to tell you that people can live healthy lives on a single kidney. And yes, you're right, I've been quite busy, so I should take some time off to relax and recover. Don't you think so?"

"If you're sure then there is no issue. Well you know we support donations to save lives, so I'm sure it'll inspire others to follow your path."

Suddenly, everybody knew Laney in Globe hospital, staff nurses came to peep in her room, "Oh! She is that lady to whom Dr. Reeve is donating his kidney." One of them commented. Joe came to know from Dr. Patil and he immediately called up Reeve. "You're a true gentleman, aren't you Reeve?"

"Only doing my duties." He couldn't understand the fuss about.

In next couple of days, all the lab tests and formalities were completed for Reeve to donate his kidney to Laney and they were ready to go in operation room. Laney hugged Reeve few times before going in operation room.

"Good luck, I'm proud of you!" Helen whispered and kissed Reeve, before he went in - only that time not to operate, but to be operated.

While Laney was having her kidney transplant operation, Rita was still waiting for a heart transplant and was in a critical condition. She was kept in intensive care unit as her vital signs were not good and were being monitored constantly. Her ECG test was showing abnormal rhythms of the heart. By evening she was complaining of chest pain. Nurse Myra immediately summoned up cardiologist Dr. Ryan Taylor. He came in a hurry and swung into action. Rita had fallen unconscious by now.

"Ventilator on." He commanded. Heart monitor beeped, giving a warning, as her rhythm started disappearing from the monitor and converting into a straight line.

"I want electric shock to be ready"

"Give me. 200" He held the defibrillator from both hands and thumped into her chest causing it tremble but no heart beat yet.

"300." He thumped again, yet no change on monitor. His own heartbeat had started increasing now.

"400. Come on." He shouted. Her upper part of body trembled again but with a heartbeat that time. Dr. Ryan looked at monitor and heaved a sigh. For then, things had come in control.

Rita's father Mr. Adam Riley, who looked older than his age with a grey beard and long hair style, was waiting anxiously outside the operation room. She was his only child. Her mother had died when she was only 12. He raced around the veranda outside the room, waiting to hear from her daughter's saviours, who were trying hard to keep her alive.

Dr. Ryan came out of the room and informed Adam that she was ok and was in sleep then.

He couldn't tell him that she was comatose. May be, just maybe, she might wake up in a few hours or in a day, he thought.

Adam waited at her daughter's bedside to see her wake up and smile. Hours and hours went by but she didn't even move. Adam checked her pulse, it was there. He shouted her name and tried to wake her up. She didn't budge. He ran outside of the room and called Dr. Ryan, "Dr. Ryan, Rita isn't waking up, what has happened to her?

"I'm afraid to say, Mr. Riley, but your daughter is in coma and we'll try hard to get her back from her sleep."

"Coma? But she is alive, Dr. – you must do something to wake her up. Please, Dr. tell me when she will wake up?"

"Mr. Riley, coma is a state of mind which doesn't react to even a painful stimuli and there is no way to tell, how long it will last. It may last one day, one week, a month or more – the fact is I don't know.."

"But there gotta be a way doctor, there gotta be a way! I mean she is alive – is there no medicine which can send signal to her mind to wake her up?

"Mr. Riley, we'll do all what we can."

"No doctor – No. This is not good enough for me. She will talk to me Dr., she will talk to me." He ran back to her room. Then he holds her hand and shouted continuously, "Rita! Rita!…This is your dad, come on wake up baby, please!" Such a sense of desperateness was new to him. He pursued and pursued, his frantic efforts to wake her daughter up - until he broke in tears and nurses forcibly removed him out of the room..

23. An Emergency

Tracey put her shirt on her shoulder from her left arm and then tried to put her left arm into the sleeve but struggled. Her right arm was plastered and left arm was already not much of a use having surgery for AV fistula for dialysis. Helen came in her room and saw her struggling, "Darling, why don't you give me a shout – maybe I can help you." Helen suggested. Tracey had broken her right arm while she lost her balance and slipped on the stairs. It was only the last steps though and yet her ankle bone was fractured. Dr. Patil had told him that due to dysfunctional kidney, her body was suffering from the lack of calcium and her bones had become weak.

"I don't want help. I want to do it myself...I'm sick of not being able to do things on my own." Tracey said miserably. In last few weeks, she has become so weak that she was not even able to stand for a few minutes, let alone a short walk. Her skin looked pale and her body structure had shrunken so much that she no more looked like a nine years old kid.

Few months back, Dr. Patil had told Helen that Tracey's creatine number was showing that her kidney had lost most of its function and it was high time for a transplant.

"It's alright darling, I'm your mother and I'll always be here to help you. Remember - one day everything will be alright."

"You always say that, don't you? Do you really believe in that?"

"Hope...darling...hope! Hope for good. That is the only thing in life which drives us all. Never give it up." She tried to encourage her.

Today they had an appointment with Tracey's nephrologist, Dr. Patil. Her labs were not good and Dr. Patil had called Helen urgently and booked an appointment.

"I'm afraid she has to be admitted, Helen." Dr. Patil said grimly without looking up.

"I thought so. Dr. Patil - look at her – she urgently needs a transplant. Is there no way she could go up in the transplant queue and receive a suitable kidney?"

"Helen - I understand your feelings. We have already placed Tracey now on High Urgency Transplant List and it's not that she is not higher up enough in queue, the problem is that her blood group and HLA types should have enough match to be sure that a transplant will be suitable and she has a rare HLA type and an uncommon blood group."

Tracey was admitted to the hospital once again. That evening, Dr. Patil went to see Reeve. He was reading some files in his room when Dr. Patil entered in the room unannounced.

"Reeve, I want to talk about Tracey. Do you have any idea how critical her condition is now?"

"I guess it's online. I've seen it."

"Oh! So you've seen her report online."

"Yes."

"Can I just add in that her condition is spiralling down rapidly and I fear, after some time her physical condition may not be good enough, even for transplant operation?"

"What do you suggest?"

"Maybe we can start a campaign for people to come forward and see if there can be a suitable donor for her."

"Good plan. Have we done this before when a patient was in a critical condition needed a transplant?"

"I guess no."

"Would we be doing this again when this type of a situation arises for a different patient?"

"I guess I won't." Dr. Patil said slowly. He truly cared about Tracey and that was the only reason that drove him to Reeve.

"Then we don't need to do this." Reeve replied.

Helen was tidying up Tracey's room when the mobile started ringing. She picked the phone up and it displayed, 'mom calling', she slides the top of the mobile slightly up and started the conversation. "Hello mom! Is everything ok?" Judy had come to hospital when she heard that they were going to admit Tracey again. She was staying overnight in the hospital with Tracey.

"It's OK now, Tracey has thrown out whatever little she had eaten in the evening but now she is OK. They have added few more pills to her 'diet'."

After a brief discussion she hung up. She never felt so weak and stalled. She felt awfully impatient; awfully helpless; as if her hands were tied behind her back and a great deal of things staring at her to be put right. Why there are things in life, I can't control? Why there are things in life, I can't do anything about? Why it's not all good about life? Why I don't have a magic wand that I can swing and make things beautiful and right?. But would that really work? Why not everything has a reason to happen in the way it happens? Gosh! Has somebody got it wrong? Does somebody need to re-create this world and re-write the concepts of life or rather re-programme us as a human being. The bloody computer gets updated every year, why not us? Why not the creator of this world, if at all exists, updates us all to make it more meaningful, to make it more responsive? She thought painfully, but of course, answers were unfounded or vague.

Reeve was studying a medical book when Helen crept in his study room.

"Busy?" She asked.

"Come in, sit."

"Judy called up."

"What did she say?"

"Tracey has been vomiting again", she paused a bit more than Reeve expected and then said, "Reeve, you have to do something!"

"Do you think I can do something?"

"I don't know. But you have to save her." She left the room, without waiting for his answer.

It had been more than a week since Tracey got admitted in hospital. As a routine, Helen was getting ready to leave for the hospital when her mobile started ringing. Reeve had already left early in the morning, as an operation was scheduled for him. She picked up the phone. It was Dr. Patil on the other end. In milliseconds of a time, before she heard anything from him, a sense of urgency to listen, to what he has to say and yet a tremendous fear of the news, he was about to break in, crept inside her. Urgency, in anticipation of a good news that Tracey has had a match for transplant. A fear, that it was some bad news about Tracey.

"I'm sorry to say Helen", Helen's heart had already started pounding, "that I've to leave for India in emergency. I know, it's a shame that she is in such a condition and I won't be here to support her case, but I've passed on all the details to my fellow nephrologists Dr. Terry Giles and I can be in contact anytime, if needed."

"Is everything OK for you?"

"My mother is critically ill and I must go."

"I understand, Dr. Patil. Please convey my regards and best wishes to your mother and family."

He loved Tracey but this time he had to go. Dr. Patil had arrived in UK almost 20 years back to do his medical degree and never could go back. He had fallen in love with Hannah who was in the same medical college as he, and married her before he could even finish his degree. His family had strongly opposed his decision to marry her and despite all his best efforts, he couldn't manage to agree them to come over to attend his marriage. Hannah's family didn't want to have their marriage in India. It was a tough decision for him to marry without having any of his family members around him when he was taking one of the life's biggest decisions. He wanted his family to be sharing one of his life's most important moments. As a protest, he had stopped communicating with his family. It was not until after two years of his marriage, he had started communicating again when one of his family friend had mediated and broken the deadlock. But in these two years, the emotional wounds he suffered in his hearts had become so deep that they left the kind of scars for which a person doesn't feel pain but seeing its ugliness in the mirror every day is a pain in itself. But perhaps every bad thing brings some positive effect as well. He had accepted the fact then, that everyone had their own perceptions of things, had their own aspirations, needs and mind-sets. You just can't change it. He remembered his marriage vows – for better or for worse…! Relationships are like that only - either you live with them for better or worse OR you leave them. *Living with them is certainly a far better option than leaving your loved ones behind,* he had decided. He had planned to settle down in India, after a couple of years of work experience, but his wife, Hannah didn't like to go to India so he had restrained his cravings to go there. He remembered the first time when they were going to India, Hannah was so excited. "I've heard so many things about India, I'm just so ecstatic." But the excitement didn't last. Perhaps the three weeks of holiday in India was too much of an asking for the classy Hannah who couldn't cope with sweltering heat, uncontrolled traffic and perhaps a weird way of doing things in India. After that trip she said only one thing to say, "Give me one good reason, why would you want to go to India, let alone settling down in India." What reason he could have given her? Living in the comfort of western world, she could be instantly forgiven to be shocked to see the mad traffic and murderous pot holes on the roads, deprived unfed beggars, freebie passengers on the roof of the trains or simply inefficiencies of the systems.

But how could he have had shown her the sense of belonging, the 22 years of cherished memories, the friends and family he left behind, the craving of going to places where he visited regularly when he was there, the craving of that road-side food stalls where he enjoyed eating for many years with his friends and families, the evening outings in shopping malls which opened till late, the fresh morning walks he enjoyed most of the year in that dry weather, the sense of confidence he felt, just by being there where he spent his whole childhood and a good part of his youth? How COULD he have? So, he kept his silence. Perhaps, it was all the same case for Hannah as well and somebody had to sacrifice, so dutifully, he did and stayed in UK for good. But that day he had to go for his dying mother and nothing could stop him from going.

The news of Dr. Patil going to India was like somebody had pushed the panic button for Helen. Dr. Patil, better known as Dr. Pill, as Tracey used to call him, cared for Tracey like his own daughter. He even used to spend his lunch time with her whenever he could. Besides he was one of the best nephrologists around and Helen was certainly feeling a sense of insecurity then, despite knowing that Reeve was there in the hospital. She called Melissa and demanded the contact numbers where she could enquire the transplant list status on her own. She had a sense of urgency that she had to take everything in her own hand and possibly she couldn't rely on anybody. But After spending couple of hours on phone, calling several numbers, she realized that she needed more than her untiring efforts, probably a bit of luck..

24. Judgement Day

Reeve arrived in the hospital at sharp 8.30am in the morning and after a brief encounter with her daughter, he went straight to work. He switched on his computer and then walked to the dispensing machine in his room and took a cup of water. The computer was ready to log him in by the time he sat on his chair. He swiftly typed the password and pressed enter. Globe Hospital logo appears on the background graphics. He clicked on an icon and opened the 'critical patients' file on his computer. There was only one name - Tracey Harvey - on the list. He wasn't surprised though. Dr. Patil had briefed him about Tracey before he left to India but perhaps he wanted Reeve to see himself that Tracey was fulfilling all the criteria of 'critical' patients.

He once again opened a software which could match a given blood and tissue sample with the samples in hospital database. He ran a search for Tracey's blood and HLA types and after a few minutes of scan, computer screen brought up the results. Surprisingly, there was a match. Rita Riley. He remembered this name. The name had been on the critical list for quite some time before and he knew that the girl was still in coma.

After spending some more time on his computer, Reeve went to see Rita's father. He knew that Mr. Riley would be in Rita's room. Mr. Riley had taken indefinite leave from his work and was spending most of his time with her daughter who was in coma. The nurses have had heard him talking to her daughter who was in deep state of unconsciousness. He read her newspapers, magazines and shared his life with her, as if she was aware of her surroundings. He even brought her dresses and requested nurses to change her dress. "She is fed up of wearing old dresses but she can't go out to buy herself, can she?" He had told a nurse. He even applied her cosmetics occasionally. She had been in coma now for 36 days and there was never a day when he had missed her bringing pink roses in the morning. "My daughter is mad about pink roses", he would proudly tell everybody. Reeve knocked the door and Mr. Riley said, "Come in". Reeve found Adrian sitting at her daughter's bedside.

"Mr. Riley. How you have been doing?"

"I'm just tired a bit. My daughter is angry with me, she doesn't talk much."

"Perhaps you would want to take some rest. Of course, we would let you know when your daughter is ready to talk to you."

"What kind of rest I'd take when my daughter is here?" He snapped back.

"Sometimes it can be hard to accept the reality."

"Accept the reality? You won't understand doctor, had it been your daughter in this stage then only you would have known."

"I agree, I don't understand."

"Yes, I'm sure you don't."

"I have come to see you on purpose."

"Purpose? What an unlucky father can do for you?"

"I want your permission to donate Rita's kidney. Her blood and tissue type is a rare match for one of my patient."

"She is not dead, doctor. Not yet. I'm not interested in signing any paper."

"Mr. Riley, unlike your daughter, who can be donated a heart only when a person has died. One doesn't need to be dead to donate a kidney. Besides, she is young and she has a good chance of coming out of coma. Most of the people live a normal healthy life after donating a kidney."

"My answer is still 'no', doctor."

"And I'll still wait for your answer till evening, Mr. Riley. Give me a shout if you need to know anything."

He came back to his room. His mind was racing at its fastest pace. He had to save her and that was the only thing weighed on his mind. Nothing else mattered.

After a while, he dialled Joe's extension. "Joe, do you have any urgent appointments for the day?"

"I've only one appointment in half an hour but otherwise there is nothing which can't be held back. Tell me?"

"Once you've finished your appointment, come to see me please? I'll be in my room most of the time or ask Julie where I am."

"No problem, see you then." Joe put the receiver back.

Joe entered in his room about one and half hour later since he spoke to Reeve. Reeve seemed to be searching for some information from a thick medical book.

"You were sounding quite hurried? What's the matter?" Joe asked Reeve.

"I want you to evaluate Tracey immediately; she is going to have a transplant surgery tonight."

"Oh! That's great news. At last we found one then…is it from a cadaver donor or living?"

"I want you to do another thing as well."

"And what is that?"

"I want you to ask me all the questions after surgery only and till then I'll tell you what you need to do." Reeve then explained further, "I want you to prepare a team for tonight's operation.

Surgeon will come at sharp 9pm in the operation room. Before that everything and everybody must be ready."

"Sounds like quite an operation?"

"One more thing, if anybody asks any questions, tell them it's being done on my order and you don't know anything. And keep reporting me your progress."

"But where is the kidney to be transplanted."

"I'll tell you but meanwhile you prepare everything else please."

"I'll do. You're the boss!"

"Appreciate that."

Joe left the room perplexed. He had never seen Reeve like that before. *He looked tense and unsure – Hmm! both the characteristics are unlike of him, but what could be better than Tracey receiving the transplant eventually,* Joe thought happily. His first reaction was to call Helen, tell her and congratulate but then he thought Reeve might not want that either. I better hurry up; there is a lot to do before 9 pm deadline. He decided.

Reeve was waiting in his room for Mr. Riley. He knew that he won't come but he ought to wait for him. He looked at the wall clock. Both hands were 120 degrees apart from each other. Small hand was pointing sharp at eight. It was time; all the visitors must be out from the hospital. *Mr. Riley must have gone now,* he thought. At 8.15pm his phone rang. He picked up the phone. It was Joe on the other side. "Operation room and team is ready – when 'donor kidney' is arriving?"

"It won't arrive."

"What do you mean?" Joe was feeling uneasy somehow. Was donor present in the hospital all the time, then why Reeve didn't tell anything? Till then, he had ignored that Reeve has not given much information, thinking it's his usual nature to speak less. *He*

THE SAVIOUR – NEVER LETS HER GO

is not a good communicator by any standard anyway, he had thought. But things were not adding up then. Why Reeve had asked him not to ask any question before surgery? The questions had started creeping up in his mind, relentlessly.

"Donor is in room 608, building E." Reeve explained.

"Rita Riley, the girl who is in coma?"

"Yes." Reeve replaced the receiver before Joe could have asked anything.

At 9 pm, in operation theatre, two beds were laid parallel to each other. Anaesthetist, Dr. Chris Tennick, had anaesthetised the patient already. The nurses were all geared up for the duty. Joe, as a physician, was a part of the team to monitor general health of the patient and the donor. They all were waiting for the surgeon to arrive as Reeve had instructed them. The room was dark except the operating area which was focused by the special halogen lights. In a few minutes, there wait had ended when the door opened and a doctor entered. He was in his operation gown and wore gloves, cap and a safety mouth cover. It was difficult to recognize, with his face barely visible in darkness of the room. "Ready everybody? Knife." he asked. Nurse Kate handed him the knives. Joe recognized the voice – it was Reeve. Why is he doing the kidney transplant, it's not his speciality? It was not like he couldn't do that, if he wants to, as he knew Reeve is known to have experience in various surgeries. But, why he was doing himself when there was a kidney transplant surgeon already there in the hospital, he thought. A wave of questions were coming to his mind, but he was not alone; everybody in that room was perplexed.

Only the area on the abdomen, which was needed for the surgery, was visible and rest of the area was covered with some special clothing. Reeve made a surgical cut on the lower abdomen of Tracey. After a few minutes of careful surgery, the kidney was ready to be removed; he then moved to Rita's bed and made an incision on the side of the abdomen to remove her kidney. After a few more surgical cuts and handling of the blood and internals, he was ready to remove the kidney. He then placed the transplanted kidney into Tracey's pelvis and connected it to the blood supply. Tracey's own kidney was higher up in the abdomen. He then connected a transplanted tube from the transplanted kidney to the bladder. The major part of the transplant surgery was complete then. He then stitched up the wounds and wrapped up the surgery. Joe was keeping an eye on the monitors which were showing the vital signs of both the patients. Everything seemed to be under control.

Reeve removed the mask from his face and came out of the operation room. He had a look of defiance; a defiance of a soldier who had gone into enemy territories knowing well that he would be captured. The operation was successful and there were no sign of rejection of new kidney yet. He felt relieved, yet he knew, next few days are going to be difficult. He had called Helen before operation, to tell that he was going to stay in hospital tonight with Tracey. He went straight to his room and sat on his chair. The clock on the wall ticked half past eleven. He felt quite exhausted but not sleepy. It was an intense operation. The next day was going to be a long day for him.

Helen reached hospital at eight am in the morning to see Tracey, unaware that a transplant operation, she was hoping for her daughter for over a year, had already taken place. Reeve had called her previous day just before the operation to tell that Tracey was doing fine but there was no indication of an operation. She had an uneasy feeling about something, when she entered Tracey's room. The room was empty, she checked the bathroom. Tracey was nowhere. Nurse Kate, who had seen Helen entering the room, came after her.

"Looking for Tracey?"

"Yes."

"She is in still in the ICU."

"ICU? Why?"

"Don't you know she had undergone a transplant surgery yesterday?"

"I know." She lied, then left the room immediately and went straight to see Tracey.

Tracey was in sleep. A drip was being transfused in her body. She gently touched her forehead and massaged her hair. How innocent, beautiful and fragile she looked and yet so much pain was being inflicted on her. She didn't believe in god, but if there was one, she surely would have hated. After a few minutes, she went to see Reeve. She didn't know what had happened. Why Reeve hasn't told her anything about transplant? Was everything OK? Her mind was racing after those questions and she knew only Reeve could answer that.

She opened the glass door and stepped in. Reeve was asleep in his chair. His computer was still on. He was an early riser and it was unusual for him to be sleeping at that time in the morning. He must have been working late, she thought. She sat on a chair opposite to him and waited for him.

Her eyes were rolling over the clutter on the table when she saw a file which holds her attraction. It was titled, "Globe Hospital Trust". She held back her urge to pick it up and peek into it. Within a few minutes, Reeve woke up and finds Helen staring at him. "When did you come?"

"Just a few minutes ago. I haven't woken you up, have I?"

"No, no but may be your smell has to be blamed."

"Is it a compliment?"

"You bet it is."

"It's a rare then. How is Tracey? Is there something I should know?"

"She is fine. She is recovering from a transplant operation."

"Why didn't you tell me?"

"It was my own decision and I didn't want to involve you or anyone."

"What decision?"

"About transplant. About kidney."

"Where did she get kidney from?"

"It came from a patient in our hospital who is in coma."

"Is there anything wrong?"

"Nothing except transplant has undergone without consent of Mr. Riley who is the father of the patient Rita."

"What? Did you talk to him about this?"

"Yes, he didn't agree."

Helen's heart had started pounding in anticipation of undesirable turn of events. "You're not telling me that you've done something illegal, are you?"

"In a way, yes, it is illegal to transplant a kidney without donor's consent." He said, as a matter of fact.

"What do you mean, "In a way"? IF, it's illegal, it is illegal." Helen felt agitated. She was frightened for him.

"I meant, saving my patient's life is legal though. Wouldn't you agree?"

"You didn't need to do that. You know that?"

"Oh yes! I needed to do that. Transplant was the only option for her and after a few days that option would have gone. The way her health was deteriorating, she wouldn't have been fit enough for any operation after sometime."

"But it's NOT morally right, is it?"

"May be not, may be it is. What is morally right for you may be wrong for me and vice versa. At times, defining moral is as difficult as defining god. Everyone has their own definition and belief.

What is morally right for a doctor may not be right in the eyes of lawmakers; what is morally right for an executioner, may not be right for a common man; what is morally right for an army, may not be morally right for a police, what is morally right for a spy, may not be morally right for a politician; what is morally right for a citizen, may not be morally right for a foreigner and what is morally right for a mother, may not be morally right for a neighbour."

"Hmm! I see what you mean. What will happen now? Does Mr. Riley know about it yet?"

"I'm going to tell him now. In fact, I must hurry – it's about 9am and he will be coming in anytime soon."

"Do you know how is he going to react?"

"I've done what I had to do. He has every right to react in whatever way he wants."

He left the room, leaving Helen alone, pondering about their future.

Adam Riley was surprised to find Reeve in her daughter's room who was still in coma.

"Dr. Harvey! Good morning! How is my daughter doing?" He asked while he put down a bouquet of pink roses on a bedside table."

"She is fine. She's as valiant as you and I believe she'll go home with you soon."

"I certainly hope so."

"Mr. Riley, your daughter is especially brave because she has saved one life even while she is in coma."

"You must be joking."

"I am not. I'm your guilty Mr. Riley."

"What are you saying? Where is my daughter?"

"She is still in coma."

"What happened to her?"

"I've donated your daughter's kidney without your consent."

Adam Riley was shocked; he couldn't believe what he had just heard. He raged with anger and grabbed Reeve by his shirt's collar, "How dare you touch my daughter?"

Reeve didn't speak. "I'll get your hospital closed for this." Adam continued.

"You may not need to do that. This is my last day in this hospital. From tomorrow, I'll have no authority in this hospital. An independent trust will run this hospital."

"You can't escape so easily. I'll get the best lawyer to see you in jail with maximum sentence." Adam retorted.

"You won't need a best lawyer either; there will be no defence from me. I'm your guilty, therefore, I must repent." Reeve assured, with a sense of certainty.

25. Repentance

The news had broken instantly that morning in the hospital. The hospital staffs were shocked to hear what had happened. The revelation made by Reeve had taken everybody in awe of its rarity and its consequences feared for the hospital, for the staffs and for their mentor, leader and the owner of the hospital, Reeve himself. The staffs had shown their full support and solidarity with Reeve, requesting him to return to the hospital. Everybody in the hospital signed a written request in which they requested Reeve to return to the hospital, which was then presented to Reeve. Reeve then had to make an appeal to the staffs, requesting them to leave him alone and not to distract themselves with this event. Globe Hospital being one of the top hospitals of the London, media interest on the story had been unprecedented and inevitable. Most of them ran the story with a crude view towards Reeve except a handful of them, who were sympathiser and more realistic in their approach. Due to extensive media coverage on the case, 'transplantation' had become a national topic of debate in political, social and elite circles of society. A criminal case was registered against him. The first hearing on the case was after two months. His home had become a workplace of some of the journalists and paparazzi, as they wanted to cover his every move and word. They were eager to hear from him – eager to see him defending himself, eager to see a disgraced doctor and perhaps a helpless father, who had stolen a kidney to save her daughter. The questions were thrown to him, from all the directions as soon as they saw him. "Doc, do you regret what you've done?" "Would you do the same thing, if it wasn't about your daughter?" "Do you recommend changes in the law about transplantation?" "What does your daughter think about what you've done?" "Why you've left the hospital - you're not proved guilty yet?" Reeve ignored the media circus and walked past, as if it never existed.

Reeve was packing his suitcase when Helen came upstairs and saw him packing. "Is somebody moving?" She asked innocently but sincerely.

"Yes, somebody has to." He replied.

"And why is that?"

"I want you and Tracey to live in peace and these paparazzi won't let you, as long as I'm here."

"Is it? Then why this 'somebody' can't be 'everybody?'"

He left the packing and turned to Helen intently, "It's about me Helen. I guess you both have to learn to live without me."

It had only been three weeks since Tracey had her transplant operation and Reeve had then left for an unknown destination and for indefinite time. Helen knew nothing would have stopped him when he believed that it was the right thing to do.

It had been eight weeks since Tracey had her transplant operation. She was getting a taste of life; of freedom; of joy, like never before. Her whole body had become like her own again. Before that it was as if, she was living in somebody else's body. She was eating and drinking everything which was denied to her before the operation, in the name of 'restricted diet'. Helen had said jokingly when Tracey had finished a carton of her favourite drink 'Jubina' within a couple of days, "Tracey, give it a break 'love', otherwise local shops will be out of stock for Jubina."

"Let it be, mom! They should be prepared for someone, who has to make up for so many lost years." Tracey had replied in an equally sarcastic manner."

Her recovery had been better than doctors had expected. Foreign kidney in her body seemed to be working perfectly fine, as creatine level had gone up to 11 which was merely 1.9 just before the operation. Dr. Patil was back from his India trip and was following Tracey's progress. He had been kept calling from India to know about her. A first few days were critical when her body was most likely to reject a foreign substance. She had been kept on heavy doses of immunosuppressant drugs. But she had recovered remarkably and her life seemed to be back on track then.

17th March'97

That day was the first hearing of Reeve's case. Though, Reeve had not returned yet from his indefinite hideout. Helen got ready to go to the court with Tracey. Reeve had neither left any contact number, nor made any contact with her in last six weeks. Joe had called Helen several times to ask about Reeve and had been disappointed. That morning when he called Helen, he sounded really agitated, "Where the hell is he that he can't even make a call?"

"Joe, I'm in the same boat as you are, you know that, don't you?"

"I know, I know, but I've given his bloody bail – couldn't he even call me once – that's typical of him. I don't know what is gonna happen in the court today?"

"Are you coming there?" Helen asked.

"Of course I'm - I have to, isn't it? Do you think he is gonna appear in the court today?

"I guess, yes!"

"Well, we'll see then."

There was a huge crowd gathered outside the court. Many of them chanting slogans for Reeve, "Long-live Reeve". Save Reeve, Save people." Reeve is our Hero" etc. etc. Many of them were the patients whose lives were saved by Reeve and the hospital staff who managed to come here, leaving essential care of the patients on the mercy of the few who stayed there to hold the helm. But there was also a section of the human right activists who were campaigning against Reeve, holding the banners and placards, "A guilty must be punished – that is Reeve." "Reeve – A kidney thief." "Shame on you, Reeve" etc. etc. The journalists have positioned themselves at all the strategic points to cover that high profile case and yet there were no sight of Reeve.

Inside the court, judge and everybody waited for Reeve. Joe and Adam Riley sat next to each other. Mr. Riley's daughter had miraculously come out of the coma; just a week after her kidney was taken and was recovering well since then. Joe had pursued Mr. Riley to withdraw his case since his daughter was getting better now. But perhaps it was too late to do so as the court had denied his request. In court's eye, it was still illegal to take someone's kidney for transplantation without signing proper documents of consent. Mr. Riley really wanted to save Reeve then. He was a changed man, perhaps his senses had come back, after seeing his daughter's amazing recovery.

Judge had waited long enough then, "I'm going to ask one more time for Dr. Reeve and then I'll issue a non-bailable warrant for him", he announced. At that time, a loud noise came inside the hearing room, tearing the doors apart. It was, as if, a riot was taking place outside the room and then the door was open wide apart. Everybody in the room looked shell shocked. Nobody had expected to see him then.

The judge ordered to start the proceedings.

"Dr. Reeve, the court had appointed you an attorney as nobody had presented you since now." Judge told him.

"I want to defend myself, Your Owner." Reeve replied.

"Are you sure about this?"

"Yes, I'm."

Judge waited for a second, as if, he was expecting somebody to speak and then said, "As per the hearing from the prosecution, this court finds you guilty of gross misconduct of your profession and breaching the trust of your patient. Do you plead guilty or not?"

"I do."

26. Living Forever

"Mom, come here." Tracey shouted from the toilet.

Helen shouted back at her, "What happened?" and ran to see her. She knew this was not an ordinary call. It has its own mysterious tone.

"Look at my pee." Tracey said.

Helen had a look down in the toilet. There were some traces of blood in Tracey's pee.

She felt desperate. Until a few months after transplant, Tracey had been mostly out of trouble, out of the sight of the doctors. But then gradually things have changed drastically. Tracey had been regularly ill and was continuously losing weight in the last few weeks. Having high temperature was a frequent thing for her. Helen was dreading if it was the sign of return of the old days. She called up Dr. Patil and made an urgent appointment for today.

"Helen - this may be more serious but we can't say anything until we see the test results." Dr. Patil explained Helen.

"What's your worst expectation?" Helen persisted.

"Most likely, this may be an infection or the gallbladder or kidney stones. However, we cannot rule out the possibility of the kidney cancer until we get the results." Dr. Patil further explained and continued, "The blood test and biopsy results will come by tomorrow. I've fixed a follow-up appointment for tomorrow at 2pm, is that suits you?"

"Huh? Oh yes." Helen was lost in her thoughts; she barely listened what Dr. Patil had said about appointment.

She called Dr. Patil next day before coming to the hospital to know about the test results but Dr. Patil requested her to come down to the hospital. She felt restless and reached the hospital, about half an hour before her appointment. Dr. Patil attended her in his room as soon as he knew she was there.

"Helen, I wouldn't want to prolong your misery, so let's straight come to the point – tests are positive for cancer but don't need to panic yet, most likely we'll be able to fix it. But we still need to do some more tests to ascertain at what stage it is? I would like her to start the medication by today itself."

Tracey was joining the pieces, one by one, of her 1000 pieces puzzle of a night time picturesque view overlooking the high rise buildings of New York. Her Chemotherapy had started last week but Dr. Patil had warned that cancer was at its quite advance stage. Helen was looking at Tracey intently, watching her every move and the preciseness that she was picking only the right pieces and slotting them together carefully. Helen's life was no different to that puzzle. Her life was torn apart in pieces and all the pieces were messed up in a heap which wasn't making any sense. Only difference was that she had no power to put those pieces together and make sense of them, like what Tracey was doing. Helen was increasingly feeling frustrated and helpless since Tracey's cancer was diagnosed. It was, as if, somebody was suffocating her life bit by bit and yet wanted to keep her alive- but just. In the last ten years, there had been no breathing space for her. She wasn't sure whether she had become more resilient OR weaker to bear all this, in those years. When she had first learned about Tracey's transplant, for a moment she dreamt that perhaps things were going to be normal for her but then she had realized that not everything was according to the plan. And when she felt happy for Tracey and thought her life was back on track, the disaster had struck. She desperately wanted to see Reeve today. She had visited him only once since he was awarded a six months jail term, a month ago by the court. I must not keep about Tracey any longer, she thought. She remembered the last visit when Reeve had asked her not to visit him in prison. "What's the problem in visiting you?" She had asked.

"Nothing that I can explain you. This is only a request." He had replied.

She walked through the aisle of prison cells. Some of them shouted on her from their cells. The atmosphere was as depressing as of a graveyard. "I can't believe this is real. Could I have ever imagined that I'll ever visit somebody, as dear as Reeve, in prison?" She murmured. In life, one should expect the most unexpected things to happen. She was learning it hard way.

Reeve was doing his daily yoga exercises when he was told that somebody was visiting him.

He was expecting her.

She hugged him as tightly as she could. "You've become weak." She said softly.

"No, I think, I've just become healthier."

"How I wish that you were there for me, for Tracey!"

"How is Tracey?"

"She is not well."

"I know but is she making any progress?"

"How do you know?"

"Mr. Riley visited me three weeks ago."

"Mr. Riley? What did he say?"

"He came to thank me for saving his daughter, before even she came out of her coma."

"What?"

"The kidney I transplanted from her daughter to Tracey had some infected cells for cancer."

Helen couldn't believe what she had heard. "What? And how this was done?"

"We performed all the required tests but it didn't show anything. I don't know - something somewhere went wrong."

"Dr Patil must know about it, but he didn't mention it to me." Helen asked.

"I think he just didn't want to complicate things for you."

"What more could be complicated than it already is?"

"Rightly said."

"You don't feel guilty for Tracey, do you?"

"I don't. Should I?

"No. Not at all. You've done what was best for her. Besides, there was not much choice. She couldn't have lived without transplant."

"Is chemotherapy working for her?"

"It's still going on. Chances are fifty-fifty."

Tracey looked herself in the mirror. Her head had turned completely bald then. Helen was staring at Tracey from her behind. It was almost unbearable for her to see at her daughter. She remembered the days when she made plaits, ponytail and different hair styles for Tracey and Tracey loved them all. Her baldness had become the most horrific reminder for Helen that Tracey had only weeks to live then. Chemotherapy had not worked. She planned to visit Reeve today. Only four weeks were left for his release from prison.

She left Tracey with Judy and drove to prison to see Reeve.

"She has only weeks to live."

"Have you taken second opinion?"

"Dr. Patil had himself arranged for Tracey to see the top two cancer research hospitals. Both have almost the same opinion."

Reeve was silent, as if nobody was talking to him. Helen waited for him patiently.

"She can still be alive, no matter whatever happens to her."

"I'm sorry?"

"I'll explain."

It had been two weeks since Tracey had requested Helen to stop all her medication. She had argued, "Mom, I've only few weeks left whether I take medicine or not, it is not gonna make much of a difference now. For my whole life, I've been on medicine. In my last time, I want to be free of medicine; of worry that whether medication is working or not; of everything. I just want to live for these few weeks."

Helen couldn't stop her. She had a valid point,

At twenty past two that day, Helen dialed the emergency number that was given to her by organ donation agency, to call as soon as Tracey had passed away. As Reeve had said, Tracey had to continue living even after her death. She remembered his words, "Arrange to donate all her organs, after she is resting in peace."

Tracey's body was lying on the floor. Helen rested her head on her lap and waited for the team to arrive. She was numb and void of any emotions; of any thought; of any physical power to react in anyway. Damn it! They say there is a god then what had she done to deserve that the ten years of her motherhood, her love, her devotion and care was taken away from her for forever.

27. A Beginning

The day of his freedom had arrived that day. The officer handed him over his belongings.

"You're free doc'!"

"I'm not a doc anymore."

"It's a shame coz lots of people need you."

"Be sure they'll manage without me."

He came out of the aisle and saw Judy and Joe were waiting for him. They all hugged each other, making a small circle, as if a rugby team was displaying their team's strength and unity. It was supposed to be a moment of pleasure and celebration, yet their faces were covered with dark sadness of somebody's loss – somebody too dear; too innocent and too young, to be lost. Joe had met him just a week ago, to inform about Tracey. While they walked out of the premises, Reeve looked around to see if there was anyone else - perhaps his eyes were searching for Helen.

Judy has sensed it already but she waited for the right moment. They sat in the car - Joe on the driving seat, Judy next to him and Reeve on the back seat alone.

As soon as the wheels started moving, Judy took out a piece of paper from her purse and extended her right hand towards the back seat. Reeve unfolded the piece of paper. He recognized the writing.

It read:

"Dearest Reeve,

I'm going away for a week, or, a month or more, I don't know. I don't know yet, but whenever I'll return, I'll return to my farm house for good – I never want to visit that place again. I've to find a way forward for my life, but please don't wait for me – perhaps, you won't. I would enjoy the suffering of missing you. May be suffering is the only way to cure suffering for me – they say, diamond cuts diamond. I wish I could be as strong as you.

I don't know why, but somehow I feel that Tracey would've been alive if you were out there. You must have done something to save her. You must have!

Forever yours,

Helen"

The car has stopped now. They walked inside the house, side by side of each other. Nobody spoke, as if saying anything won't make any sense. They enjoyed each other's company, for a while, without speaking much and after that Joe left the house.

Judy and Reeve sat down for a tea. After a while, she spoke, "I'll have to leave for farm house in about an hour – it's urgent."

"I understand, thank you."

"You don't need to say."

"I know."

"What you plan to do for living now?"

"Anything. Anything, which is labour intensive and would be just enough to fill my stomach, twice a day. Do you suggest any job for me?"

"I can't think of any, for a man of your talent. Why don't you spend some time on farmhouse?"

"I'll plan. By the way, you keep an eye, if any of your clients need a helper for their horse yard."

"Are you serious?"

"More serious than ever. I'll clean the yard, take care of the horses and will do everything needed to be done."

"You can work with me then, can't you?"

"No, I can't. I won't be able to do justice with my job."

"Alright, I've a client. Be sure, you've a job, any day you want."

"I can start from tomorrow."

"Are you sure?" I'll see what I can do and give you a call."

"I'll wait for your call."

Judy was gone after a while. The house had the silence of a graveyard. The wall in the living room was full of large posters showing several pictures of little Tracey. He lied down on the couch, carelessly, staring on those large posters. She was taking her first step, her first meal, her first smile, her first experience on the toilet seat, her first drink from the beaker, her first crawl on the bed, her first step on the stairs, her first journey in the plane, and her first journey in the train. She was sitting in the bath tub, the white foam covering her head and face, making a funny shape. She was happy and smiling in her school dress. She was riding her tricycle. She was jumping with Joy in a bouncy castle. She was sleeping and smiling in her sweat dream.

It was surreal to look at her and difficult to perceive whether her life was captured in the images or the images had become alive.

"She never lived, never died, she was always there", He spoke to himself. He could not feel the weight of his body, his legs or his arms. It was a sheer shallowness he felt in his body; his heart and his mind. But he could hear the noise of his heart pumping the blood.

No, I am still breathing. The show must go on. Let's tomorrow be a new beginning. He deliberated.

A flow of wind swung the curtain inside through the open window.

He felt the wind and its cooling effect on his wet eyes.

A new sense was born to him.

His sixth sense.

Her spirit.

AVINASH AGARWAL

Printed in Great Britain
by Amazon.co.uk, Ltd.,
Marston Gate.